PRAISE FOR M. B. GOFFSTEIN

"Goffstein is a minimalist, but her text and pictures carry the same emotional freight as William Blake's admonishment to see the world in a grain of sand and eternity in an hour."

—*Time* magazine

"M. B. Goffstein is one of the finest illustrator/writers of our time. Like porcelain, there is more to her work than meets the eye. Beneath the delicacy and fragility is a core of astounding strength."

—*Washington Post*

"A book by M. B. Goffstein is a beautifully simple and simply beautiful thing."

—*New York Times Book Review*

"One of the few modern author-illustrators who are assured classic status."

—*Publishers Weekly*

"It's good to have a Goffstein! She unearths the treasure of simplicity."

—*New York Times Book Review*

THE COLLECTED WRITINGS OF M. B. GOFFSTEIN

Words Alone: Twenty-Six Books Without Pictures

Art Girls Together: Two Novels

Daisy Summerfield's Art: The Complete Flea Market Mysteries

Biography of Miss Go Chi: Novelettos & Poems

BIOGRAPHY of
MISS GO CHI

M. B. Goffstein

BIOGRAPHY of MISS GO CHI

Novelettos & Poems

DAVID ALLENDER PUBLISHER

DAVID ALLENDER PUBLISHER
is devoted to the work of author-artist,
M.B. Goffstein (1940–2017).

David Allender Publisher, New York

Back cover photograph by Tanya Bylinsky Fabian

ISBN: 978-1-949310-06-1
e-ISBN: 978-1-949310-07-8

we love your work, & we'd like to meet you.

CONTENTS

BIOGRAPHY of
MISS GO CHI

The Mildred Stories

Days and Nights at
Our Prairie Home

Alvina listens to the radio, hoping to hear one of the jokes she sent in to her favorite show.

Her sister, Lillian, washes the dinner dishes.

Lillian's husband, Bernard, is out on the porch with the cat, Long John Silver.

TEN-YEAR-OLD MILDRED looks at herself in the mirror in Alvina's room, and hopes she will be like her Aunt Alvina.

WITHIN THE first half hour of Alvina's coming to live with them, Mildred brought in her doll Inez, and Alvina exclaimed, "Oh, for cute!"

Once, when Alvina dropped a dish, she said, "Oh, for crying in the beer!"

SOMETIMES LILLIAN is as grouchy as a bear to Alvina.

Lillian isn't used to having someone at home with her all day long.

She likes to take a nap in the afternoon.

She wants Alvina to get a job, so she reminds Alvina that she taught grade school before she married Bernard.

Since Alvina had to stay on the farm because Lillian went to Teachers College, she says, "Go kiss a fly!"

Alvina laughs so hard at her own wit that Lillian tells her, "Laughing makes you fat."

LONG JOHN Silver takes a sip of milk.

MOTHER AND Aunt hear Mildred's step on the porch.

It was Instrument Day at Mildred's school, and she brings home a French horn. She has signed up for lessons.

Alvina wishes she could play a musical instrument.

The accordion would be her dream, playing schottisches and polkas at weddings and dances.

BERNARD COMES home from the Sewing Machine Company.

Dinner is on the table.

After the dishes are done, the family gathers in the living room.

At the piano, Lillian plays and sings "Annie Laurie."

Alvina surprises Lillian by singing harmony: "Gave me her promise *true*, which ne'er forgot shall *be* . . ."

BERNARD BRINGS a typewriter home from his office, and encourages Alvina to take a typing course at Night School.

Alvina signs up for World Literature.

One night she dreams there is a giant cockroach under her bed. She screams in her sleep.

Her Night School class was reading a story in which a man became a beetle.

Lillian tells Bernard that World Literature is wasted on Alvina.

WHENEVER ALVINA gets on the bathroom scales, she sings the "Too Fat Polka."

WHEN MILDRED goes up to her room, she imagines a beautiful little horse waiting for her.

BERNARD AND Lillian have a quiet moment together.

ALVINA WRITES down the day's weather in her diary.

Up at the Lake

A picture of King Edward VIII in Mildred and Alvina's room at Presidents Lodge shows how far north they are—almost at the Canadian border.

Bernard says, "This is the life!"

His wife, Lillian, keeps her eye on the cake cart, waiting for it to come around.

A STRANGER named Veronica joins them. She has been out bird-watching.

Lillian asks Bernard if he brought their binoculars from home.

Lillian introduces their daughter, Mildred, to Veronica.

Mildred attempts to win the Lodge game: get the ring on the stake in the jug.

Veronica shows her how it's done.

LILLIAN'S SISTER, Alvina, has been out at the workshop behind the Resort, talking with the handyman, Joe.

Another guest, Betty, enters the Lodge. Mildred thinks Betty looks like a Hubba-Hubba Girl.

Betty is married to a sailor, and she advises Alvina to marry one, too. "They can sew," she says.

But Betty guesses that Alvina likes Joe, as he measures a new drawer for the desk in the Lodge.

THE DINNER bell rings, and Veronica leads the way to the dining room.

"There you are, Larry!" Betty says to her husband.

She calls teasingly, "What are you waiting for, Alvina?"

The presidents' portraits are in the dining room: Washington, Jefferson, Monroe, Jackson, Van Buren, Tyler, Pierce, Fillmore, Buchanan, Lincoln, Johnson, Grant, and Hayes.

"Not all the presidents are here," Lillian tells Mildred.

"Maybe they're still in their rooms," says Alvina.

"Maybe they're riding around the lake," says Larry.

JOE IS leaving tonight. He waits for Alvina in the Lodge after everyone has gone to bed.

Alvina's heart is pounding as she looks in the mirror one last time.

Mildred is asleep in the other bed.

Alvina thinks Joe wants to elope with her, but he just says he is no good at writing letters.

Alvina cries as Joe says goodbye.

IN MILDRED'S dream, Alvina is voted Queen of Presidents Lodge.

Her humble subjects await her command.

She chooses Joe as King. God bless them!

Boiled Rice Mountain

to my cousin Mary
with love

Part One

Excelsior

Mildred Vikla grew up thinking she was her Aunt Alvina's illegitimate daughter.

She knew her father and mother, Bernard and Lillian, weren't her real parents. Lillian said she had asked at the dime store for a little girl with blond curly hair, and they gave her an Indian.

By the time Mildred knew her suspicions about Alvina weren't true, she was confirmed in her single life.

She liked buying her own popcorn and eating it at her own pace.

She didn't like discussing movies. She liked letting the characters live in her head.

Antoine Doinel, Antoine Doinel, Antoine Doinel from *Stolen Kisses* was still in there.

She was fifty-nine and would leave, when she died, a few household furnishings, clothes, books, and notebooks.

Mildred lived the way she thought the Native Americans had lived: without a trace.

THE PHONE rang in her small, spare apartment in Excelsior, Minnesota.

"Mildred Mary?"

"Who is this?"

"A voice from your past."

"Eddie?"

"How are you?"

"I'm sorry about Bea."

"How do you know?"

"It's in the paper."

She could hear Eddie pouring a drink.

"I just opened her safe-deposit box. When can I see you? I'm in Minneapolis. There's a letter for you."

"A letter from Bea?"

"And two manila envelopes with your name on them. There's also a date on each, September 6, 1953. I think there's a lot of money inside." The glue on the envelope flaps was brittle with age and Eddie had peeked inside.

"Why would Bea leave me money?"

"She liked you."

Eddie poured more scotch.

Guests

1953

Bernard received word that his only brother, Lewis, was in the hospital.

Lillian refused to go to Detroit Lakes unless Alvina came to help her clean his apartment.

"Can Mildred stay with us?" asked Bea.

Bea and her sons, Dean and Eddie, moved next door to the Viklas when Mildred and Eddie were nine.

Bea used to sit on her porch holding a wrinkly *Life* magazine and fantasize that the Viklas would die, leaving Mildred in her care.

THE GREAT day finally arrived.

Mildred had a little metal clicker. "I can't talk," she said. "When I do this once, it means yes. When I do it twice, it means no."

LEWIS VIKLA'S apartment was spotless.

"Don't stay there!" he cried from his bed at the V.A. "Stay at Presidents Lodge!"

He was so happy to see Bernard and family, he called and made the arrangements.

Abe and Gertie Washko, the owners, were card sharks like the Viklas.

Their handyman, Joe Denton, told Alvina his real name was Dayton.

His father owned Dayton's Department Store.

He was doing this to show the old man he was responsible enough to inherit his money.

Before he met Alvina, he didn't know if he wanted to be that rich. He talked to her while taking out the trash, sweeping the floors, and emptying ashtrays.

Joe showed her repairs he had made that were written up in magazines.

He advised his father about Dayton's, told him to sell sporting goods, and look how that went.

It wouldn't have surprised her that he was fired from Dayton's for stealing, but she liked hearing him talk as he went about his sad work, or the sad work he made of it.

The Washkos wanted to adopt him and leave him Presidents Lodge.

Did she see that portrait? The Washkos didn't have that president, so he painted it.

He had replaced fretwork on the Victorian facade. That was hard, he admitted.

Joe must have thought Bernard was rich, because he said he was leaving and asked Alvina to come with him.

He told her to meet him that night behind the Lodge and be prepared not to have it so good.

He stole some carafes.

"I bet he thought they were silver," Gertie Washko said, slapping down the cards.

IN MOUND, Bea showed Mildred her art books.

"They have better fireworks at Excelsior," Mildred said, on seeing Whistler.

Bea opened the Renoir. "See that big dog? Is one of those girls your age?"

"No."

"Doesn't your mother look like Madame Charpentier?"

"No."

She turned some pages. "Isn't that a cute little dog?"

"She shouldn't kiss him on the mouth," Mildred said.

"You're going to have my room." Bea took her upstairs.

"Look!" Mildred said.

She had found Bea's only treasure, a party favor from a lunch for her cousin Bonita.

Bea held out her hand.

"It's so cute!" Mildred said.

"We used to say 'cunning.'"

She didn't like the way Mildred was holding it—and her hands were dirty.

Bea felt wrung out.

The boys never acted this way. She just loved them and told them to behave.

She expected more from a girl: sympathy, understanding, even compassion.

She had kept the little cake for twenty years, and it was an antique when she got it.

As Bonnie's best friend and first cousin, she got the plaster cake with white icing and colored candies.

"Can I have it?"

"No."

"Can I play with it while I'm here?"

"No. It's precious to me."

Mildred's tiny nostrils flared.

BEA DROVE the children to the Buckhorn, anxiously peering out at unfamiliar roads.

They arrived safely and sat in a booth under old license plates and joke cards.

She let Mildred order shrimp, make a face when she tasted it, and order a hamburger.

She gave them change for the games.

After a game of driving up a dangerous highway, Eddie came back to the booth.

He had Bea's father's square jaw and pink complexion and even wore his hair like him.

Dean had a heart-shaped face, an olive complexion, and long green eyes. He carried a comb to keep his sleek dark hair slicked back with water.

At eleven, he was shorter and slighter than Eddie.

Eddie wore khakis belted at the waist. Dean's denims rode his slim hips.

Eddie liked shirts with crisp sleeves and collars.

Dean, the sleeves of his white T-shirt rolled up over an imaginary pack of cigarettes, was looking after Mildred.

"My sons are true gentlemen," Bea thought, her eyes welling with tears.

"Mom?" asked Eddie.

She waved her hand at the upside-down sea of cigarette smoke.

CLUTCHING THE handrail, Bea slowly went downstairs, carrying sheets and a nightgown.

She was going to sleep on the sofa.

"Is everything all right?" Sheriff Bud Craig called through the screen. "You were gone a couple of hours?"

She wearily let him in, and they sat on the porch and looked across the lake.

"I tried to show her some of my art books," she said.

"*Oh-h, oh-h,*" they heard from somewhere out in the dark.

"Is that an owl?" she asked.

"No."

"Oh-h, Brian."

"I thought they said, *'tu-whit tu-whoo.'*"

They laughed, embarrassed by the sounds that seemed so close.

"Do you have a flashlight?" Bud asked, knowing that if she did, she would never find it.

He went down to his car, came back up, and went down the hill and all the way to the lake, thinking, "Damn that deputy of mine."

When he got to the shore he could just make out a boat being rowed away.

THE NEXT morning Bud Craig drove to the drugstore and parked his cruiser.

"It's okay," a pretty girl called to him from the perfume counter, "I got over you."

Everyone could hear her.

"Elsa, I didn't see you."

"Thanks a lot!"

"How are your folks?"

Bud used to see them regularly when he dated her.

Laughter coming from the soda fountain made him cross the aisle and look over the top of the magazine rack.

Ivy Iverson's face was flushed with excitement.

Stella Hurok was humped up on a stool, her skinny little legs dangling, her big face alive with interest.

Bunny Lasker, as bald and dented as a celluloid doll, said, "You're only young once."

The door opened and Brian La Rochelle came in.

Bud took him back outside and said, "I'll only say this once. *Oh-h, Bri-an.*"

"What?"

"Weren't you on West Arm last night?"

"No, I helped my mom clean the garage!"

Mrs. La Rochelle walked out of the dime store.

"Ask her," he said.

Bud put out his hand, gave Brian's a shake, and took him back inside.

He said to anyone listening, "Brian wasn't on the lake last night."

Bud sipped his coffee, thinking, "I know that was Mary Catherine's voice."

Brian, timidly blowing on his coffee, knew someone had committed a crime and the criminal looked like him.

He put a nickel on the counter and left.

Bud stayed where he was and soon had the pleasure of seeing Bea and Mildred.

Mildred climbed up on the stool next to him.

He said, "I hear you had an art lesson."

"Art lesson?" She contorted her little face.

"I thought Bea—Mrs. Ashton—was showing you some of her books."

"She's going to get me a comic."

"She's so nice."

"I might get an *Archie Annual*."

"Don't do that," Bud said. "They cost twenty-five cents!"

"I know, but they're funny. Did you hear Mary Catherine Ottie pretend to be kissing Deputy La Rochelle last night?"

EDDIE ASHTON got an A- for writing this:

> *Our sheriff is kind to criminals. He washes and irons them himself.*

His teacher wrote, "Don't you mean the secondhand clothes he collects for them, Edward?"

> *He says if you look sharp you feel sharp and then you can be sharp.*

I think he is better than minsters ["Spelling!"] who say
what their best friend God wants.

"An excellent, thoughtful paper," Miss Helbig wrote. "Bud Craig is kind to everyone, not just criminals."

A Letter

2003

Hearing Eddie's voice brought back images from Mildred's childhood.

> *Your boots above the road*
> *Your green glacier eyes*

While paying her bills and cleaning her apartment, she worked on two lines about Dean.

Weekdays she got home at six, bathed, got ready for bed, made herself a sandwich, and worked on her poems. The hours went by in a flash.

As she waited to fall asleep she would work on a problem and solve it.

"YOU LOOK the same," Mildred said.

"You too. You look great, Mildred."

"How's Dean?"

"He's fine. How's your Aunt Alvina?"

"She's fine. She's married to Ray Sims."

"Who?"

"He drove the Greyhound bus she took to work."

Mildred's mother's maiden name was Similink, so Mildred had been worried that Ray and Alvina were related.

"How're your parents?"

Bernard had a stroke after lakefront property skyrocketed, and he sold their place for $1 million.

"He died, but Lillian's fine."

"Are you married?"

"No, are you?"

He had bought her a briefcase at the Fendi shop in his hotel.

"Someone would be more apt to steal this than the envelopes," she said.

She plotted her life like a crime, wearing plain but expensive clothes.

Each season, she bought five or six separates at Dayton's, wore them to work, and gave them to the Salvation Army at the start of the new season.

When a coworker commented that she never wore jewelry, she bought diamond earrings, waited for winter vacation, and had her ears pierced.

Eddie hadn't touched his steak. He had downed three or four drinks.

"Does Dean drink as much as you?"

"Tell me about yourself. No one's a secretary anymore. They're administrative assistants. Are you an administrative assistant?"

"Yes I am," she said, laughing.

"Aren't you going to read Bea's letter? I want to know what it says!"

September 6, 1953

Dear Mildred,

You may not remember me by the time you read this.

I hope it will be a long time from now, because I want to live a long time.

I hope we will have been friends all these years and that you won't be surprised to hear from my lawyer.

I bet you think I am leaving you a book.

From the time I moved next door to you, I wanted to be of use to you.

What I am giving you belongs to you, but you wouldn't have it if not for me.

This is what I do as a teacher: give people the use of their own gifts.

When you were nine, you saved the life of a mobster.

He had a certain courtly charm. But, Mildred, gangsters are killers. I hope you stay away from them.

I was watching for him and intercepted him as he limped down your hill.

The money he gave me for you is sealed, dated, and addressed to you.

By the way, I know you took my little cake, but that's okay, because you do take the cake!

I like to think you still have it as a souvenir of our friendship.

    With love,

    Bea Ashton

MILDRED LEFT a message at work that she was taking a personal day.

"Alvina," she said, "did I ever save a gangster's life?"

Surprise

1953

Bernard had a surprise for his family. When they got to down-town Minneapolis, he drove inside a building and stopped beside a little house.

He rolled down his window and a man in the house gave him a ticket.

They drove up a ramp and saw rows of parked cars.

"Go around again," Lillian said, but Bernard was going up to the second tier.

"Don't go any higher," she said.

"I can't help it!"

He parked on the fifth and highest tier.

At the elevator, he put their ticket in a slot, hit a handle, and the ticket was stamped "5."

They rode down to the ground floor and walked over to the auditorium.

When they were in their seats, Bernard bought programs and hot roasted peanuts.

The woman next to Lillian pointed out Patsy Ann Buck's mother and father, saying, "They live down the block from us in Saint Paul."

Patsy Ann skated onto the ice wearing a powder-blue costume, her blond hair in a page boy.

Her powerful thighs crisscrossing backward, her white shoe skates dazzling the ice, her tiny skirt fluttering over her rear, sometimes flipping up to show matching panties, she went into a spin.

Faster and faster she spun until she was just a blur. She crouched spinning with one leg out.

Still spinning, she started to gain height, raising her arms and spinning more slowly.

"I bet you wish you could skate like that," the neighbor leaned over and said to Mildred.

A man came down the stairs selling dolls on sticks.

"Dad!"

Bernard reached for his wallet.

Her doll had fluorescent pink feathers and a glittery blue top hat. Sawdust, peanut shells, and popcorn littered the floor. Cold air emanated from the rink, and from the rafters came cones of colored light and gay skating music.

Mildred looked adoringly at Alvina's low bumpy nose and small mahogany-colored eyes.

A man and girl skated out in Czechoslovakian costumes. The man lifted his partner high above his head, swooped her down, and whirled her above the ice.

Lillian's eyes sparkled like the spangles on the costumes they wore. None of the girl skaters had the figure she once had.

"Popcorn?" asked Bernard.

"They feed that to pigs," said Alvina.

"I love popcorn," Mildred said.

"Come skate with me, la, la, la, la," Lillian trilled along with the music.

When they got to the parking ramp, Bernard consulted his ticket, pressed the elevator button, and up they went.

"Elllll."

"The one from Iowa fell!" Alvina said.

"What do you expect?" Lillian asked, getting in front.

"Elllll."

Alvina got in back. Both doors closed on the passenger side of Bernard's Oldsmobile.

"Get in," he said to Mildred.

"Someone's in the trunk of that car!"

"No they're not."

"Elllll."

"Get in!" he yelled.

"No!"

"I said get in!"

"Who is it?"

"Who cares!"

"Elllll."

Lillian leaned over and rolled down Bernard's window. "What's the problem?"

Bernard opened the back door and tried to push Mildred in. He hurt her.

"Stop it!" she screamed.

Lillian got out.

Bernard shouted, "Get in and let's go!"

"Aaaaagh!" Mildred screamed, hoping Bud would hear her. "Help!"

But Bud had parked on the street, and he and Bea and the boys were eating at White Castle.

A police car roared up the ramp.

"What's going on?" the police chief asked Bernard.

"She's just tired."

The chief said to his sergeant, "I'd hate to hear her when she's not tired!"

They drove off.

"Elllll."

"You heard him, Dad!"

Mildred screamed again, and the chief drove back up the ramp.

"What's going on?" he asked with feigned weariness.

"There's a man in the trunk of that car!"

The chief loved mobsters. Thanks to them he was living his childhood dream.

"You folks have to leave," the chief said.

Bernard, Lillian, Alvina, and Mildred went back to the car and opened their doors.

Alvina's big bones, dark red hair, and brown eyes reminded the sergeant of an Irish setter who befriended every child in the small town he came from.

"You have to leave the car."

It was 11 p.m. Patsy Ann Buck whirling like a top on the glittering ice was forgotten.

The sergeant asked, "Would you folks mind going out and getting a hamburger or some pie and coffee?"

"Get the works, our treat," the chief said.

This wasn't getting the trunk open. "Go on, now—get!" the chief said.

They got in a cab.

Bernard sat in front with the driver.

THE OFFICERS had reinforcements and a light explosive.

The young sergeant retched when he saw Sally Lamartino's legs encased in cement.

As they hauled him out, he memorized the license of the dark blue Olds before he fainted.

BABE BEECHNUT, Julie Mulestine, and Shorty Shortino drove up to the fifth tier and saw an Olds parked next to the car Shorty was going to drive to Lake Calhoun.

Julie and Shorty got out, their hands on their pieces.

Babe opened his door, ready to fire over the roof of the Olds.

The first shot rang out.

Julie and Shorty were killed. Babe was wounded and taken into custody.

The young sergeant lay on the oil-spotted floor.

The chief held a cigarette to the dying man's lips, so the gallant young man who never smoked used his last breath to take his first puff.

IN MOUND, at 9 a.m., Bernard called the parking garage.

"It's the owner of the blue Oldsmobile," the employee told his boss.

"Oh, boy."

"Mister, you better come get your car. You already owe sixteen bucks."

"I'm out in Mound," Bernard said. "I'll take the bus."

"You don't plan on driving the car back, do you?"

"Sure."

"You can't drive that car."

The boss grabbed the phone.

"Tell me how you can drive with a busted motor, busted windows, and no door on the driver's side!"

Bernard dialed the police and gave them hell.

"Maybe we can pay for the parking," the desk sergeant said.

Bernard yelled, "You'll pay for the whole goddamn thing!"

He called his insurance agent, and Mr. Krantzas took him to Minneapolis.

A LITTLE GIRL SAVED MY LIFE

Mobster Salvatore Lamartino spoke highly of a young lady who argued in the parking ramp with her father until police came and opened the car trunk he was locked in, he said today from his hospital bed.

Severe as Lamartino's injuries are, they cannot dampen his spirit.

"Mobsters are no good, but some police are no good, either," he said, citing payoffs that this newspaper will be investigating.

Part Two

Counting Chickens

1954

Mildred waited with Alvina until the bus came into sight. Then Alvina crossed the highway, said hello to the driver, and took a seat a few rows back.

"Going to work at the drugstore?" Ray Sims, the driver, called.

"Yah."

The high-back seat felt luxurious.

"I never see you at the dances over in Spring Park," he said over his shoulder.

"I'm not much for dancing."

"There's a fellow who plays real good polkas. He's a real good accordion player!"

Alvina was wearing a white cotton blouse and dark blue skirt.

As they dipped down and flew up the highway past white-and-black guardrails on the left and the Saga Hill grocery on the right, he sang "Blue Skirt Waltz."

Old Mrs. Ulrich across the aisle shyly kept time, rubbing a worn white-gloved finger on her purse.

"ALVINA AND I are collecting these chickens," Mildred told Bud Craig, taking him out to the porch.

"How many have you got?"

"Eight." She made one peck his arm. "Do you want to hold him?"

The poppy-seed eyes were glued to a pompon. The beak was the tip of a green cocktail toothpick.

"I wish I could get more for Alvina." Mildred looked at Bud intently, like a little dog or cat.

"Where is Alvina?"

"I don't know!"

"Where're your folks?"

"When I know how many we can get, I'm going to make them each a little bed."

"You're such a cute kid. I wish I had a little sister like you."

"You could marry Alvina, and I could live with you."

ALVINA AWOKE in the dark. Herbie was sleeping in the little room off the kitchen.

He'd arrived the night before, wearing his sailor uniform and carrying his ditty bag.

How Lillian had cried and hugged him. How Bernard gripped his hand!

At Mildred's request, Herbie sat down at the piano and played "Dark Eyes."

Alvina stole over the stairs to the bathroom and washed up.

The gifts he brought were displayed on the living room sofa: a card shuffler for Lillian and Bernard, a Brownie camera for Mildred, and a sterling silver charm bracelet with a sterling silver charm of California for her.

Alvina put on her best dress and black suede flats.

Later that morning, Judge and Mrs. Parks saw Alvina and Herbie at the drugstore.

"Is that her boyfriend?" asked Mrs. Parks. "He sure is good-looking."

The judge knew everything. "He's her brother. That's why they're both Similinks."

"This Is Mildred"

2009

After graduating from Mound High School in 1961, Mildred got a job as a file clerk at the University of Minnesota. She lived at home and took the Greyhound bus to work.

A photo showed her and a Beat named James Francis outside McCosh's bookstore in Dinkytown.

Francis went on to California.

In January 1962, Mildred took a Greyhound to New York.

"This is something I gotta do," she wrote to her parents. "Ciao, bambinos."

She stayed there for four months, working as a file clerk at Columbia.

Pat Fulmer, Mildred's boss, took her to films by Akira Kurosawa, Jacques Demy, and Jean Renoir.

Pat, who looked like a model, was putting herself through film school.

She cooked dinner for Mildred one night, in her tiny galley kitchen up near Columbia.

She told Mildred she could audit any class and encouraged her to take poetry writing.

Professor Roseboom read her poems and told her to read *The White Pony* and *Greek Lyric Poetry*.

He advised her to go home and get the free education she was entitled to.

He would write to his friend Berryman about her.

Bernard mailed her a ticket. She left from Idlewild. It was her first plane trip.

Jimmy Francis, Pat Fulmer, and Professor Roseboom had been angels set in her path.

Back then there were fewer people, and three angels could be assigned to her.

Roseboom lost the little poetry notebook she made for him.

It still bothered Mildred that her old poems were out there somewhere. Mildred never knew, but the unsigned poems sat in a cardboard box for nearly thirty years until they were discovered at a flea market in New York City.

MILDRED WAS in her apartment planning a vacation around visiting the used bookstores of Seattle. Driving time was about twenty-four hours.

She would offer to take Alvina, but Alvina would be bored.

Her message light was blinking. She pressed the button.

Alvina's voice told her Lillian had died in her sleep.

Mildred went to work the next morning, and no one knew she had cried half the night.

"SOMEONE OUGHT to say that she was beautiful. It wasn't just her features. It was her spirit. To use her own word, she was 'peppy.'

"She liked being complimented on her looks, and she loved clothes and jewelry."

Poor Mildred broke down.

"Sit down," she heard Cherry Sims tell her Hollywood boyfriend, Ricky Anderson. "You didn't know her!"

"I can still talk about her!"

Cherry was Mildred's cousin, Alvina's daughter. Born in California, she became a singer on TV.

"I wish I knew the words to that song, 'I Enjoy Being a Girl,'" Cherry said.

The mourners laughed, and she led them in singing "America the Beautiful."

Ricky's publicist told him to attend. As an actor, he truly felt bereaved.

Leaving the church, Mildred saw a crowd of young people scream in the stars' faces.

They got in their limo and left, rather than cause another scene.

"THAT WAS a real fine eulogy," Bud Craig said, holding Mildred's arm as they walked down the church steps after the service.

"Bea died," he said in a weak voice. "Do you ever talk to her boys, Dean and Eddie?"

"No," she said, because Eddie never asked about him.

"You remember Bea left and went east when they were still just kids. A real shame, I'm still real sad about that."

Bud paused for breath and looked at the houses across the street. There was a time when the elm trees hid them from view.

"I liked what you said about Lillian. I wish you would talk at my funeral."

AMONG THE papers Alvina gave Mildred was a mounted photo of Bernard on a pony. In it he had curly blond hair.

He was bald the whole time Mildred knew him.

"YOU DON'T want this?" Alvina held up a brown-and-yellow vase that had been on the living room mantel.

"No, but I wouldn't mind finding my charm collection."

"Lillian gave it to Cherry."

On the floor of Lillian's closet Mildred found a ball of fluff and crumpled wire.

"HERE'S LILLIAN'S watch and Bernard's watch and his papers. And a box of your old school papers Lillian kept. What are you looking for?"

"Was I adopted?"

"Your real name is Violet Martin. A man gave you to Bernard. You should have heard Lillian scream when he brought you home.

"You had $14,000 in your diaper."

That was all Alvina knew.

AT NIGHT, in motels in North Dakota and Montana, Mildred worked in her notebook.

> *Jingling their charms*
> *the pretty debutantes*
> *went in to lunch*
> *At each place setting*
> *a miniature*
> *plaster pastry*
> *might have pleased*
> *Queen Mary.*
> *How cunning, they cried*
> *One girl kept hers*
> *for twenty years*
> *till a poor little*
> *neighbor girl stole it*

In Seattle, carrying some books she had bought, Mildred passed a small shop for rent.

The owner was inside.

MILDRED LEFT her car in Seattle. When she got to Minneapolis, she called Eddie.

She said, "I have over sixty cartons of poetry books in my storage locker."

If no one came to the store, she could sell the out-of-print titles on the internet.

By supporting what she believed in, she had made a good investment.

MILDRED WALKED to the lectern and said, "Good manners kept World War II veterans from talking about their service.

"They were like ghosts. I remember being surprised that my dad could spell.

"These ghosts raised angry children. We can only hope that future generations will be stronger and finer.

"Bud Craig didn't marry or have children. He was our hero, and yesterday I learned he got a Bronze Star for gallantry in the Pacific.

"He didn't have the star or the citation, and we may not be able to get a copy of it, because the archive in Saint Louis burned down.

"It's on his separation paper, and I will only add: To a kind and handsome man who kept us safe, we say farewell."

MILDRED PRINTED a hundred labels and called UPS.

Her landlord let her break her lease. She had been a model tenant for thirty-five years, and he had a long waiting list.

At the university, Dean Brinkma was badly shaken but agreed to let her leave right away.

MILDRED FOUND a blue Mexican clay bird Jimmy Francis had given her, and almost threw it out with his framed passport photo.

He stared at her solemnly.

In Seattle, two friends happened to meet on the street.

"I hear you rented it. What's it gonna be?"

"I don't feel so good. Just a tall cappuccino."

Ed Raven realized he was taking Augie to Starbucks. "I meant, what kind of shop is it going to be?"

"Oh say, I didn't mean to make you treat me! It's going to be a poetry bookshop."

"So the wheels will still be turning." It had been a bicycle shop.

"Don't tell me you like poetry!"

"I do," Ed said after a while. "Who's renting it?"

"A woman from Minneapolis. And now it turns out you like poetry."

Ed wasn't doing much since he retired from the police force.

"What does she look like?" he asked. He was also a widower.

"There's nothin' wrong with her. How come you like poetry?"

Chief Raven thought for a while. "I like thin books. Want a croissant? I feel like you did me a good turn."

Mildred's furnished apartment looked out on the Pacific Ocean.

She hung up her clothes and, opening her notebook at the blond wood table, wrote:

> *Boats, boats*
> *Poets in boats*
> *Baby poets*
> *Rocking*
> *Angry poets*
> *Rowing*
> *Serene poets*
> *Floating*
> *Old poets cry,*
> *No shore!*

MILDRED'S BOOKSHOP, Boiled Rice Mountain, had freshly sanded floors and new steel bookcases.

Mildred was taping a handwritten sign to the window when a gray-haired Native American knocked on the door.

"Good name," he said. "'On Boiled Rice Mountain I met Tu Fu wearing a big sun hat.'"

She sold him her copy of *A Place in Space*, but wouldn't let him see what else was in the cartons.

Laughing at some comment he made, she locked the door after him.

Big Bomba

When Mildred Vikla died (honored in some circles for her much-anthologized poem "Boats, Boats") most of the gang from Mound was in heaven.

Her mother, Lillian, said, "I didn't know you liked poetry."

Suddenly, nonexistence yielded to existence and Lillian was gone, leaving a brightly lit trail.

"A man was here looking for a woman who he says had a big bomba," Bernard said. "It's not so simple. It's not as simple as it looks. You see with the heart, not with eyes."

Everyone was a soul, a spirit, a colored glow with a little light in its center.

Zillions burst and were gone.

It was like the ocean. There was no ceremony, no punishment, no judgment.

There was no recourse when a light went out.

There was no pain, no pity for a feeble light with very little gas. New lights flicked on.

Lillian was back in a flash.

She had been born, given the name Sonia, grown up, gone to college, majored in English Literature, veered into late twentieth-century art history, earned her doctorate with a thesis on the sculpture of Daisy Summerfield, and had the honor of cataloging Summerfield's papers at Princeton.

Sonia wrote in a lively style for an academic.

Describing Summerfield's last year in Mound, Sonia referred to her as "the glamorous eighth-grader."

In one sealed carton, Sonia found valuable old ceramics, bronzes, and dime-store junk collected by Summerfield.

Summerfield's favorite books included *The Hurricane of 1938 on Eastern Long Island* by Ernest S. Clowes, *Blonde Like Me* by Natalia Ilyin, *Geraldine Belinda* by Marguerite Henry, and *And I Shall Dwell Among Them* by Neil Folberg.

This and many editions of the novels of Henry James seemed to prove the young doctor's thesis that Summerfield had a strong interest in narrative.

Among the papers, Sonia liked a 1953 news clipping congratulating Summerfield on winning a statewide drawing contest for the Minnesota State Bird, the goldfinch.

She also liked a manually typed letter from Pocket Books, dated June 22, 1954:

```
Dear Miss Summerfield,
Your letter written to Jim Kjelgaard, the
author of BIG RED, has been forwarded to us by
the Teen-Age Book Club as we are the publishers
of Comet Books.
    We agree with you that the illustrations
of the Irish setters could have been very
much better, and we appreciate your taking
the trouble to write to us of your opinion.
Unfortunately, we are no longer publishing
Comet Books, so the chance that BIG RED will be
reprinted is highly unlikely.
        Thank you for your interest.
```

Sonia was thrilled by a slam book made by Summerfield circa 1996.

It was a new primary source for Alan and Daphne Kodaly, Jack Katz, Lulu King, and other art-world figures.

And there was a mystery. Among Summerfield's papers was a manuscript book, a little notebook, identified by Sonia as early poems by Mildred Vikla. This opened new avenues, and unanswered questions, for scholars. Had the two women known each other?

What scholars couldn't know is that Daisy Summerfield found the unsigned poems inside a little notebook, with a pink-spotted red paper cover, at a Manhattan flea market.

In Mildred Vikla's papers at the University of Puget Sound, Sonia found a brown spiral notebook, 8 1/2" by 7", written in purple ink in a well-developed backhand. It was definitely not Vikla's.

Summerfield had tried several handwriting styles in her youth. Could it be?

We were leaving for the airport at six! Somehow we got ready, and somehow we got into the cab, and to the airport.

There we checked our baggage. We were only 35 pounds overweight! Then our flight was called, and we went into our plane, a Stratocruiser. We sat there for at least half an hour before the signs went on and the men began to turn the propellers. Then our huge plane began taking off on the runway. We were going to Chicago and from there we would board a Super Constellation and make a nonstop trip to Miami. The trip to Chicago was uneventful. We were flying 12,000 feet above ground and our plane had a 14,000-horsepower motor. But our trip to Miami was different! Our nonstop flight became a one-stop flight, and we landed in Atlanta, Georgia. From there we took the first plane we could get, a DC-4, that wasn't pressurized. My ears hurt terribly and neither chewing gum nor cotton helped. So after that terrible trip, everyone was very relieved and happy when we made our last bumpy landing in Miami Beach! We checked our baggage, only to find that one suitcase had been left behind in Atlanta, and would be here tomorrow.

Today we visited the glassblowers. Their demonstration was very interesting! Bohemian glassblowing is handed down through the family from generation to generation. You can either be born, or marry, into a family of glassblowers. There are no books or lessons on the art of glassblowing, so I'm very disappointed in my father and grandfather for not being glassblowers! They make all their objects over a small fire. If the object is taken from the fire before it is finished, it will break!

"Excellent!" said "M. M." in a sharp blue pencil on the last page.

But this vacation assignment had been written by Paula Nathanson, whose grandparents sold their summer home to Bernard Vikla.

Lillian found it and mistakenly put it in a box of Mildred's old school papers that she never opened.

Mildred had never met Paula or Daisy, but those two had been roommates in their first year at Dewey College. They lost touch after, although the Osgood and Paula N. Conrad Bequest at the MoMA included three Summerfields: a limestone Witness, *Gettysburg*, and two Dwellings, *Haunted Room with Blue and Black Plastic and Metal Chair and Rusty Dotted-Swiss Curtain*, and *Sandstone Ark with Cotton Curtain (Red Flowers on Turquoise Ground) and Maroon and Blue Velvet Covered Stones*. The connection has yet to be discovered.

One night after working at the Widener, Sonia was hit by a car, leaving her parents, husband, and child.

Her singleness of purpose had made her careless in stepping off a curb that snowy night.

She was back in heaven before most people knew she was gone.

HEAVEN IS where stories come from, for those who spend their time on earth listening and writing them down.

Mildred heard the original of her poem "Boats, Boats."

It went,

> *Live in boat*
> *die in boat*
> *no one knows*
> *spirit boat*

And Mildred learned her secret. She was born Violeta Lamartino, daughter of Blanche Lamartino, a relative of Sally, the man in the trunk.

Boats

1954

They decided on secret nicknames.

"Lucky Strike" and "Gumball" did a good job of sanding and painting the old rowboat Bernard had given them.

One of the oarlocks was loose, so they bought larger screws and made it tight.

They oiled the mechanism that held the anchor. For their birthdays, Bea bought them life vests and an outboard motor.

They rode all around West Arm, including Jennings Bay, where hidden from sight, Dean smoked.

They begged Bea to let them go to Forest Lake.

She said they could, if they turned off the motor and rowed through the channel.

"You don't have to," Eddie explained. "You just go real slow."

"You can do that when you've had more practice."

So they rowed past the Viklas' and around the point.

It was quiet under the bridge. Smelly green water lapped the cement sides.

They emerged into Forest Lake and brought in their oars.

Dean stepped to the back of the boat, wound the rope, pulled, rewound it, pulled, rewound it, pulled, it caught, and they were off!

They saw trees, lawns, and houses. They saw Marie Krantzas' mother pinning wash on a line.

Next they wanted to go to Hart's Cafe. They showed it to Bea on the map, at the far end of Wayzata Bay.

"How about Curly's?" suggested Bud.

Bea looked angry, and he said, "All the kids use boats."

Bud talked to Bernard. "Potato Chip," tied into an orange life vest with a dollar in her pocket, was allowed to go with them.

"There's something doing between him and Mrs. Ashton," Bernard said.

Lillian's eyes flashed and her small mouth crimped. Bea didn't even wear lipstick!

EDDIE AND Mildred reached for a post, grabbed one, and held on as Dean climbed out.

He tied the boat to a post.

When Curly took their order they told him about a Chris-Craft riding very low in the water.

Curly told the water warden about the suspicious boat. The warden removed its cargo, and mobster Sally Lamartino would be buried on dry land.

"My Old Man's an Old Ex-hood"

At the University of Minnesota, many years later, Nick Lamartino was writing his doctoral thesis on Robert Lowell.
He wanted to write about his great-aunt, Mildred Vikla, but his advisor wasn't supportive.

Nick really wanted to write poetry himself. He had read the Prologue and Epilogue to Twayne's *Robert Lowell* (second edition) so many times, he had memorized some parts.

To be honest, he liked its author, Richard J. Fein, more than he liked Lowell. He had made fun of his cousin, Amy Lowell. Nick loved her poem "Thompson's Lunch Room—Grand Central Station: Study in Whites" in *Men, Women, and Ghosts*.

"What to do, what to do," thought Nick.

I can help you, said Mildred. *"What to do, what to do" is your voice. Try . . .*

> *That's my boy*
> *That's my dad*

Someone was helping him! Ecstatic, Nick went on.

That's all we ever said to each other.
I'm a young English instructor
and he's an old ex-hood
on Sheepshead Bay
Which when you think about it
Has an ominous sound.
Sounds ominous,
don't it

Leave it, said Mildred. *You'll get it later.*
He had a poem!

He was exhausted.

When you get it right, the words lock into place, said Mildred.

Light

You begin writing a novel by placing two fragments together.

As you find, clean, assemble, put aside, and reassemble fragments, a generation passes.

Suddenly the man who is looking for the woman with the big bomba says, "Here's my missus!"

He is accompanied by a merry orange glow.

The Lorraines in Hollywood

to my cousin Dorey
with love

Part One

At night, in my dream, I stoutly climbed a mountain,
Going out alone with my staff of holly-wood.
A thousand crags, a hundred hundred valleys—
In my dream-journey none were unexplored
And all the while my feet never grew tired
And my step was as strong as in my young days.
Can it be that when the mind travels backward
The body also returns to its old state?
And can it be, as between body and soul,
That the body may languish, while the soul is still
    strong?
Soul and body—both are vanities;
Dreaming and waking—both alike unreal.
In the day my feet are palsied and tottering;
In the night my steps go striding over the hills.
As day and night are divided in equal parts—
Between the two, I get as much as I lose.

—"A DREAM OF MOUNTAINEERING"
PO CHÜ-I
written when he was seventy, circa 840 AD
translated by Arthur Waley

Man and Mountain

L oretta Lorraine hadn't given her husband time to change to civilian clothes before she told him they were moving to Hollywood. He had served in the Marines for eleven years and sent home good pay.

He rose to the rank of first sergeant and served in the occupation of Japan.

One day, early in 1953, a shopkeeper stopped him on the street and showed him some scrolls.

"You buy," he insisted.

Cesar bought the seven scrolls and took them home on his transport.

NOT LONG after they moved from Mississippi, Loretta got a small part in a picture.

A fool in a spotted ascot pulled her to him and crushed his lips to hers.

She pushed him away.

"Oh, Chummie," she cried, "can't we be chums as your name implies?"

Cesar and Jane sat in the dark watching their wife and mother's image flicker.

Shortly after that, Loretta left. Her nearly grown son and daughter found their own bungalow, and Cesar took the scrolls to Berkeley.

A bookstore owner told him they were poems by Po Chü-i, also called Po Lo-tien.

They were fine old copies of a selection of Po's poems by a gifted calligrapher.

"I don't need to tell you the Japanese dug Po," he said. "Dig *The Tale of Genji*!"

Young men in jeans and plaid shirts tried to teach Cesar Chinese. They also knew Japanese.

They said it was easier to translate Chinese into Japanese and then into English.

The young men were poets. They loved the mountains and Zen Buddhism.

MONTHS LATER, back in Hollywood, Cesar found a hut on a mountain owned by Mrs. Van Islip.

She would gaily call from her car, "Yoo-hoo! I brought a picnic!

"May I enter?" she would ask.

Wafting delicious perfume, she would tiptoe around as if in a museum.

"Tell me about this," she would say, stepping back from it with her hands clasped in front of her. "There must be a story behind this."

"Yes, it's my teakettle."

WHEN MRS. Van Islip was murdered, she took it lightly.

As her bereaved son and daughter, Mark and Linda, flew to L.A., their mother was making the trip to heaven.

She wondered if she should go back and tell the police to quit wasting their time. Should she just tell them her lawyer killed her?

She knew that her children loved her and were very upset right now.

"Oh, let the police look," she thought, losing interest as she continued her lone journey.

Alone in his hut and unaware of the murder, Cesar sat translating a poem by Po Chü-i.

He realized that the pavilion under the bridge was really a reflection in the water, and the moon was the "silver-haired intendant" who hadn't changed in fifteen years.

Someone knocked at his door. It was Segal, Mrs. Van Islip's lawyer.

"You've had it pretty good," Segal said. "I want you off my property now."

As a Taoist, a Buddhist, and to a lesser extent a Confucianist, Cesar accepted change.

Po Chü-i was often banished, so Cesar packed his books, his scrolls, his bowl, his kettle, and his little stone Buddha, and started down the mountain.

The Girl in Black Velvet

J ane Lorraine combed her bell of brown hair and colored her lips
Adorable Red.

Dogs As I See Them by Lucy Dawson lay open on her bedspread.

She dropped the lipstick in her bag, went out the door, hopped into
her old gray DeSoto, and sped off.

Jane and Faidoh Lorraine shared a bungalow in a neighborhood of
little California cottages, each with its palm tree, its orange tree, and
two jasmine bushes, all practically on top of one another.

In the house next door, Dorey Deane poured skim milk on her
granddaughter's breakfast cereal.

She couldn't find the little girl.

As she knocked on Faidoh's door to see if she was there, Tippi
jumped up from where she was hiding in the back of Jane's car.

She had put on her best dress.

"I'm going to be a model like you."

"EEEEK!" Jane screamed.

Jane had to stop, take her by the hand, go into the office of a service
station, and ask to use the phone.

"Do you know your number?"

The youngster didn't know her grandmother's number, so Jane called Faidoh.

Dorey Deane was glad that Tippi was with Jane.

Instead of going home and eating her cereal, Dorey let Faidoh make her a plate of deep-fried pastries called beignets, and chicory coffee with cream.

As a child, Dorey and her cousin made up stories with their paper dolls.

"Writing was like that," she told Faidoh.

"Give me cardboard characters!" she said.

As you told the story, themes began to emerge, and even the plot made sense.

Now she was the author of the Jack Danger series, hard-boiled detective stories, and was about to be fired.

Danger hadn't solved the last two crimes.

He kept going into bookstores and telling clerks he was learning Russian. He began collecting quilts and bronze Hagenauer cat figurines from Rena Rosenfeld's shop in the Waldorf.

Dorey indulged herself by quoting poetry, her own and others'.

She liked to bring back old characters that she felt comfortable writing about. But she'd change details about them from previous books and get complaints.

The many readers who identified with Jack Danger, Private Investigator, were being disappointed.

Her boss, Abby Sundell, was hinting heavily that it was time for Dorey to take on something different, a series called The Grizzled Miner.

The poor miner didn't have another name, and he didn't solve crimes.

He came into town or went up in the hills, and things happened.

L.A. is a city of stories. Everyone wants to write, direct, and act in stories.

Above all, they want to live their own stories as writers, directors, designers, and actors.

They bring their talent and beauty to L.A., the city that believes in stories.

Driving aimlessly, Jake Hirsh, the movie producer, had a problem.

He had bought the rights to an article in *Life* magazine about a sculptor, but Jake couldn't find the right girl for the love interest.

He wasn't interested in artists. As Jake read the article, he had a vision of a young brunette, a beauty, in a dark alley wearing a black velvet coat.

He needed someone very special, bright and simple. An unknown. Someone, somewhere, with that special something.

On a whim, Jake parked and went into a drugstore for a cup of coffee. And there at the counter was the girl, wearing a black velvet jacket, Jane Lorraine.

JANE HAD had a busy morning.

After taking Tippi home to Dorey, she had sped to work. She had parked her old DeSoto and hurried into the studio.

"Relax," said her best friend, Carole Camell. "The stylist isn't here yet."

Carole Camell was a tall and elegant young blond, the sole support of her widowed mother.

Taking out her compact and opening it, Jane was chagrined to see her hair had puffed out.

Carole was always cool and collected. Her blue eyes twinkled at her friend.

Jane tried to smooth it.

"You're a darling," said Carole.

"I love your dress," Jane said.

"I love yours!"

The stylist came in.

Hours later, Jane and Carole went across the street to a drugstore for a cup of coffee.

That's where Jake Hirsh saw them. As he stared at Jane, he realized she wasn't wearing black velvet at all. She had on a dark plaid dress by Claire McCardell with a deep leather belt.

His mistaken impression had been a vision, a sign, and Jake knew his search was over.

Segal Makes His Move, Loretta Gets It Wrong, and Jane Gets Her Wish

n his long trek down the mountain, Cesar recited an Arthur Waley translation of Po Chü-i:

> *I have never battled to buy a fine house,*
> *I have never fought to own great lands.*
> *What I had to fight for, having got a place of my own,*
> *Was to sit tight for more than ten years.*
> *I turn and look at the houses of the Top Clans*
> *Lined up in the heart of this great town—*
> *White walls flanking red gates,*
> *Splendidly staring across the wide streets.*
> *Where are the owners? All have gone away . . .*

"I'LL JUST familiarize myself with Mrs. Van Islip's will before the kids get here," Segal said.

He sat behind the desk in his former client's study, waiting for Linda and Mark Van Islip to arrive.

Segal opened the will and clutched his chest in surprise.

"Oh, my goodness!"

"Wha'?"

"I'm just so amazed and touched!" He stared at his secretary.

"Wha' happened?"

"Ilah Van Islip left me her mountain!"

"She couldn't have." His secretary snapped her gum. "You're her lawyer."

"But remember that document you witnessed? The one that was covered by a blank sheet of paper so we couldn't read it?"

"That was the mountain?"

He vowed, "Her name will live forever in my housing development on Islip Mountain."

"That's a good one."

"MARK, LINDA." As Segal stood to greet them, he felt like their elder half brother.

"My condolences," he said, leaning forward to kiss Linda, who quickly stepped back.

From the anteroom outside the study, he heard a man ask for him.

"You can't go in."

Segal was surprised that his secretary defended him.

"Why not?"

"He's reading a will."

"He can read it to me," the man said.

Mark and Linda seemed fascinated.

"What do they care," he thought. "They're rich, protected from the world.

"It doesn't matter that they aren't good-looking, have lousy personalities, and have no sex appeal."

He was ready to take out his gun and shoot them, when the police walked in.

Mark went over to Segal, took the will from him, and started reading.

He said, "This is wrong. Mother willed the mountain to Cesar Lorraine."

"Brisky, Bronzino, take him away," the plainclothes detective said to the two uniformed cops.

Segal was stunned.

As they led him out, he thought, "These fools are so rich, they let their mother give away a mountain!

"That's not all!

"They want to see that 'Mother's wishes' are carried out and the right person gets it!"

"Looks like you had the right hunch, detective," Brisky said.

"Just hit me out of the blue," the detective said.

THAT EVENING, Jane had to work late. Faidoh combed his hair high off his forehead and into a neat DA in back, crossed the street, and rang the bell.

Erna Laing had been a sultry black-haired silent film star but now she never worked and lived alone. Faidoh was sure she was lonely.

She came to the door wearing a kimono and marabou-trimmed mules.

"Yes?"

"I was wondering if you like catfish. I fried some for dinner. If you don't have other plans, will you share it with me?"

"Ain't it terrible there was a murder," Miss Laing screeched. "I been scared to go outside!"

"Yes, ma'am," he said, holding her elbow and looking both ways.

THEY SAT down at the table and clinked glasses.

He had never seen anyone eat so fast. He was afraid she had been starving.

"Can I give you a helping to take home?"

"All right. What kind of work do you do? You could be a chef," Miss Laing said.

"Right now, I cook and take care of the house for Jane. But I've been thinking about becoming a Private Investigator. It sounds pretty interesting."

"Don't you have a girlfriend?"

"The girl I like is called Margie. She's so cute. She's the police chief's secretary, but he's never there. She really runs the place."

"I seen her," Miss Laing said. "I thought you was going to say you like your sister's friend.

"Even she ain't as pretty as your sister, who I saw in the paper Mr. Hirsh is going to make a star."

"Is that right?" Faidoh said. That was news to him.

"She's the type they want these days. They call it The Girl Next Door."

AFTER FAIDOH walked Miss Laing back to her cottage, she was still excited about her evening out.

She walked into her bathroom and looked at herself in the mirror.

In her own eyes, she was still beautiful. But why was her hair so flat? It made her eyes look frightened.

"I'm scared to be old and ugly," she whispered.

THE SAME night he met Jane and Carole, Jake Hirsh had planted a piece in a gossip column, hoping the brush with fame would entice Jane to call. She had been aloof, surprisingly cool, when he told her he could make her a star.

Like Miss Laing, Loretta Lorraine always read the gossip columns. "Jane?" she thought. "Louella Parsons always gets things wrong."

Loretta finished dressing with her usual care and took a series of buses.

"Name," said a studio policeman.

"Miss Lorraine."

"Go right ahead."

Jake Hirsh threw open the door of his office only to be disappointed.

Loretta graciously thanked the guard who escorted her from the building.

Her children had invited her to live with them, and it wasn't their fault she didn't drive.

But she blamed them as she stood in the hot sun waiting for the bus.

A PRIZE-WINNING German shepherd puppy, son of champions, was delivered to Jane.

The card said, "I know you prefer this to flowers. Let's make a movie, J. Hirsh."

She called his office, trembling with emotion.

Her call was put through.

"So when can we start?" he asked.

"I can't leave him!"

Jake hadn't thought of that reaction to his gift and could only say, "Enjoy," as coldly as possible.

The puppy's ears flopped. His legs were as thick as two-by-fours. He had tiny sharp nails and teeth.

His little eyes were intelligent.

He squatted and wet the floor.

"No," Jane said. She scratched the door, took him out, and cried, "Good boy!"

The puppy thought, *That makes sense. Everyone has to live here.*

He chewed everything in sight.

She named him Chewy, after Po Chü-i.

As she praised him and held him to her side on a short lead, he thought, *She is good to me. When I grow up, I will be her brain.*

JANE CUT back her work schedule to two days a week.

"I can't fly to New York," Jane told the fashion editor at *Harper's Bazaar.*

"Why ever not?"

"I have a dog."

"Can't someone take care of it?"

"No."

"What kind of dog is it?"

"*He's* a German shepherd. He's named after Po Chü-i. His other name is Po Lo-tien."

"You can take him with you."

"I don't want to go!"

The exasperated fashion editor, Noli Long at *Harper's Bazaar*, couldn't believe what she was hearing. She cried, "WHAT ARE YOU?"

"White, Indian, and Negro."

"Oh, my dear! I never—I didn't mean—I would never—Did you say Indian?"

NOLI LONG and the photographer and his assistant and the stylist and her assistant flew to California.

Jane liked Mrs. Long because Mrs. Long liked her.

"Oh!" cried Jane, standing in her slip and looking at some photos.

"What is it, my dear?"

"I love that dress."

"Then you shall have it. It's a Fox-Brownie. I'll give you a carton of their frocks."

Noli usually sold her old clothes, but these weren't hers. Anyway, they were American, not French.

She phoned her office in New York and told them to send the Fox-Brownies.

The garments were casual and charming. Now she had insight into Jane.

> JANE LORRAINE. The All-American Girl. White, Indian, and Negro.
>
> Her beloved German shepherd—Polo—named for an ancient Chinese poet, goes with her everywhere.
>
> Her hobby is collecting clothes by American designer Stella Brownie.

They were giving her a personality, making her a star.

In the spotty, breathless style of the magazine, on seemingly casually designed pages, were histories of three French artists, with postcard-size reproductions of their work and Jane modeling the clothes of French designers.

The Givenchys, Diors, and Mainbochers came by plane, costing a fortune in overweight.

The article was a sensation. Noli was always right. Everyone knew that.

Pure Land

Days after the murder, footsore and weary, Cesar Lorraine arrived at Faidoh's door. They sat together on the steps.

"Papa, I have bad news. Mrs. Van Islip is dead."

"Ah."

"She left you the mountain in her will, but we can't pay the taxes, so you can't accept."

"Please pour us out a little wine, so I will tell you a story. In my cabin I want to light my stove, but there are no matches. All night I shiver."

"Papa!"

"Next day I go down the mountain and buy matches.

"Then one day I open a book and find some matches that were there all the time.

"So the question is, what if you have something and you don't know you have it."

Suddenly Cesar's soul started to leave his body.

Faidoh, holding his precious father to him, heard him gasp, "Is that Erna Laing?"

Miss Laing had dressed and gone out. She was coming home carrying a grocery bag.

"Non, non, non," Cesar cried, freeing himself and rushing to her.

God is good to us.

As our looks fade, our eyes dim.

Cesar saw her as she appeared in silent films when as a boy he went into town from the bayou.

He helped carry her bag and she thanked him. The way she spoke English was music to his ears. It sounded like Chinese.

As the poet Li Shang-yin said, "To see her shadow, to hear her voice, is to love her."

THE STORY of Mrs. Van Islip and the mysterious man on the mountain was big news. The newspapers thought he was "Caesar Lo Rein," a Cuban, or Cuban-Chinese.

His stern visage appeared on magazine covers at the drugstore.

Erna Laing became famous again, due to his reference to her "moth eyebrows." She had been separated from her husband, a rancher in Oklahoma, but the publicity helped them reconcile.

Paramount Pictures offered Cesar a contract. The studio bought The Grizzled Miner for Cesar and gave Miss Laing the role of Miss Louie.

Instead of satin gowns, she wore crisp cotton dresses by Louella Ballerino.

Thanks to her boss, Dorey Deane, the new writer of the series, became a consultant.

For the film, Dorey wrote the famous scene in which Miss Louie serves the Grizzled Miner a sandwich.

The look on his face as he hesitates to pick it up in his dirty hands would win him an Oscar.

CAROLE CAMELL and Jake Hirsh were married after a whirlwind courtship.

Carole thought, "Why not?" Jake was so in awe of her all he did was tease her mother.

Her mother, Ada Camell, once told a bobby in London her name and he said, "Surely not the whole thing?"

Now, Jake would ask how she seasoned it.

Carole was seeing a psychoanalyst because she didn't understand him. He was the one who needed analysis!

MARGIE ASKED Faidoh to come to her high school reunion as her date. She wore a navy-blue jersey Claire McCardell dress, a gift from Jane.

"You look fabulous," her friends exclaimed, as the band played old songs.

They played "Ballerina," "I'm Looking Over a Four Leaf Clover," "Mañana (Is Soon Enough for Me)," "Now Is the Hour," "You Call Everybody Darlin'," "Cruising Down the River," "If I Knew You Were Comin' I'd've Baked a Cake," "Hoop-Dee-Doo," "Harbor Lights," and "Tennessee Waltz."

They were saving "Goodnight Irene" for the last dance.

They played songs that came out after this class graduated: "Be My Love," "Wheel of Fortune," "Kiss of Fire," "I Went to Your Wedding," "Don't Let the Stars Get in Your Eyes," "Till I Waltz Again with You," "Song from 'Moulin Rouge' (Where Is Your Heart)," "Oh! My Pa-Pa," "Little Things Mean a Lot," "Three Coins in the Fountain," "Sh-Boom," and "Mr. Sandman."

And they played new songs: "Let Me Go, Lover," "Sincerely," "Dance with Me, Henry," "Unchained Melody," "Rock Around the Clock," "The Yellow Rose of Texas," "Ain't That a Shame," "Love Is a Many-Splendored Thing," "Autumn Leaves," and "Sixteen Tons."

Just as the last notes of "Goodnight Irene" faded, Faidoh asked Margie to marry him.

CESAR'S MOVIE earnings more than covered the taxes on the mountain.

For a moment Cesar did think of building a Genji-style compound for his family.

But roads would be bulldozed, trees uprooted.

Why go to any trouble, when these nice little homes were already built?

CAROLE ARRANGED a beautiful wedding gown of white-on-white tissue silk tartan.

Jane, the maid of honor, chose to wear a dark plaid taffeta tartan.

Carole couldn't see herself in tartan, so her gown was matte blue stripes on white silk.

All three of them were carrying bouquets of sweet peas with bright ribbons.

Faidoh and Cesar wore navy-blue suits, white shirts, and striped ties.

Faidoh made the cake.

The entire Los Angeles police force was bringing their spouses or dates.

The fire department wanted to know how many invites they could have.

Chief Conger would give Margie away. He and Mrs. Conger were staying in town briefly for the wedding.

ELSEWHERE IN the Universe, when Ilah Van Islip saw the Pure Land, she felt something try to enter her consciousness.

But she no longer remembered Cesar Lorraine, who would have liked to know it existed.

Part Two

[WRITTEN IN EXILE]

At night I dreamt I was back in Ch'ang-an;
I saw again the faces of old friends.
And in my dreams, under an April sky,
They led me by the hand to wander in the spring winds.
Together we came to the village of Peace and Quiet;
Yüan Chên was sitting all alone;
When he saw me coming, a smile came to his face.
He pointed back at the flowers in the western court;
Then opened wine in the northern summer-house.
He seemed to be saying that neither of us had changed;
He seemed to be regretting that joy will not stay;
That our souls had met only for a little while,
To part again with hardly time for greeting.
I woke up and thought him still at my side;
I put out my hand; there was nothing there at all.

—"DREAMING THAT I WENT WITH LU AND
YU TO VISIT YÜAN CHÊN"
PO CHÜ-I
translated by Arthur Waley

Love and Dust

J ake's wife, Carole, had a very moody husband on her hands.

Producer Jake Hirsh needed Jane Lorraine for his next movie, *Love and Dust*. The *Harper's Bazaar* article convinced him more than ever that she was a star. But Jane wanted to spend time with her dog—one that he had given her!

"Jake, why not just write a part for a dog?" Carole asked. "Then Jane could take him to work."

"Don't be ridiculous!"

Love and Dust was based on a *Life* magazine article about a sculptor, Alberto Giacometti.

Later at the studio, Jake met with the scriptwriter. "So what if Giacometti's girlfriend has a dog?"

"You mean like the mice in Cinderella?"

"No, just a friend. Maybe with a medical condition or a limp so we get the warmth."

ELLEN, THE dog trainer, took Chewy into a soundproof room, read him his lines, and discussed his motives.

"Action!"

"Chewy, what's wrong with your paw?" cried Jane.

I'm acting.

"Cut!"

Chewy passed his screen test with flying colors.

JAKE'S MOOD didn't improve.

"Now we have to see if *she* can act," he grumbled to his wife.

Jane got tips from her father's cameraman, Mr. Killman.

"I can't act," she told him.

"It's better. Go up to your mark and say your lines. Do what the director tells you to do.

"You do have to think, though. 'What should I have for dinner' can look tragic.

"Ask your dad."

"He says it's like the Marines."

"WHO'VE YOU got for the male star?" the studio head asked.

"Gene Kelly."

"Kelly?"

"He's the right height, and he speaks French and Italian. Put him in a frizzy gray wig, and he even looks like Giacometti."

ALBERTO, A rich and famous artist, lives in squalor.

The camera travels through his place in Paris: the bedroom with a chair for a night table, the telephone room, his studio, and his brother, Diego's, studio.

Alberto's studio is gray, and guests leave covered with the dust of clay and plaster.

A museum director is coming to choose work for an important retrospective.

Annette has an idea.

As soon as Alberto leaves for the café wearing a short necktie, she starts dusting.

"BLACK-AND-WHITE?" CRIED Jake's boss.

"It's a study of the artist as killer."

ALBERTO SITS in the café tabac surrounded by admirers as he draws on a napkin.

When he comes home and sees what Annette has done, he is furious.

He is superstitious about the dust. He wanted it. "Look what you have done," he says.

"You have ruined me!"

"Let me put in a dance," Kelly said.

As Giacometti comes in and sees what Annette has done, he advances on her:

Jeté sauté, jeté sauté. Jeté, jeté, jeté, jeté. Changement, changement, changement.

He says his lines and leaves.

"I'd like Annette to imitate him," Kelly said.

The director didn't mind. He told the cast, "Let's see where Kelly takes this."

Kelly did Jane's part.

Everyone loved it.

She had to stay late and work with him. He had taught children to dance.

Standing in third position, she would sweep her right leg behind her left leg, sweep it out, and hop on it.

Then the left leg.

Sweep it back, sweep it out, hop.

Sweep it back, sweep it out, hop.

Then the sweeps without the hop: right, left, right, left.

Get in fifth position, jump high in the air, change the feet in midair, and come down in fifth position.

ALBERTO STORMS out. The dog limps over and Annette talks everything over with him. Annette decides to leave Alberto.

Everyone thought this called for a song. A contract musician was called in.

"Can you sing?" Kazan asked Jane. If not, he would teach her to sing-speak the words.

"Yes," she said.

"You make it hard to love you, something like that," he told the songwriter.

"It should be Peggy Lee singing about a dust devil," the songwriter thought. "They could have cast her and dyed her hair."

ALBERTO DOESN'T come home that night. We see him with some ugly customers.

Now does Annette stand in the alley?

Jake just realized that the vision he had carried in his head, the vision that tormented him as he drove around Los Angeles wasn't in the movie.

What he had was a Gene Kelly musical in black-and-white directed by Elia Kazan, who didn't do musicals.

"What have I done?" Jake moaned.

The limping dog and Jane's beauty weren't saving the picture.

"It's all Carole's fault," he told his psychiatrist. "She made me think Jane was so special."

"What did I tell you?" the psychiatrist said.

KAZAN HAD to go back to New York. He was directing a play on Broadway.

"Goodbye and good luck," said Jake.

"We're taking out the song and dance and going back to the earlier script," Jake told the cast.

"You're cutting the good stuff!" Kelly said.

"It wouldn't be worth cutting if it wasn't good. It will add to the strength of the movie."

Kelly's appeal to the studio head fell on deaf ears.

ANNETTE DOESN'T leave Alberto. The Giacomettis go to London.

Alberto moans he has done nothing, his work is no good, he shouldn't be showing it.

He buys Annette a black velvet coat.

We see him at his opening surrounded by rich bohemians and intellectuals.

He returns to Paris. Annette stands in an alley in her black velvet coat.

JAKE'S BOSS learned that Giacometti was a real person.

Jake said, "We changed his name to Umberto Raspelli. Her real name's Jeanette."

"We're gonna get sued," said Jake's boss. They only acquired rights to the magazine story, not with Giacometti.

"It's loosely based on him!"

THE CREW watched the dailies.

"What's the girl doing in the alley?" the writer asked Jake.

"She feels secure around dust bins."

"She could hear a kitten, save it, and have something of her own," someone said.

"She already has a dog," someone else said.

"Art is the real religion," thought Jake. "The right thing always comes from it."

IN THE alley, Annette's dog limps toward her and falls over in a faint. She rushes him to a kind veterinarian.

Annette leaves the dog with the vet in London.

But standing in the alley behind Alberto's studio, she decides to return to the dog and the handsome young vet.

MGM's EDITOR was in Europe when *Love and Dust* was completed. Released to third-rate theaters, it was booed by winos in Times Square when Jane didn't undress.

The high-collared black velvet coat looked so promising.

Artists and out-of-work actors in the daytime audience thought it was great.

A weird cat, Raspelli, was a sculptor, and his beautiful girlfriend posed for the crazy plaster gargoyles he modeled in clay.

It infuriated the winos that he modeled her head and she wore a blouse and skirt.

The artists and actors watched the credits:

Directed by	ELIA KAZAN
Raspelli	GENE KELLY
Nanette	JANE LORRAINE
Director of Photography	MARTIN KILLMAN

There were all kinds of gaffes.

Jake wanted it fixed, but the studio didn't care since it was making money.

The part where Raspelli brushed one foot behind the other and brushed it out was too much!

Word of mouth spread. Middle- and upper-class matrons berated their local theater managers.

"Listen here," they said. "We depend on you to give us the important shows. We want *Love and Dust*."

Same Ch'ang-an Moon

Cesar sat reading "On His Baldness," a poem by Po Chü-i, translated by Arthur Waley:

> *At dawn I sighed to see my hairs fall;*
> *At dusk I sighed to see my hairs fall.*
> *For I dreaded the time when the last lock should go . . .*
> *They are all gone and I do not mind at all!*

Cesar had almost completed the second year of his seven-year contract with Paramount.

To please him, they were making a film of *The Life and Times of Po Chü-i*.

Honey Levine and Honey Shapiro had read the book.

"Po Chü-i and Yüan Chên were hardly ever together!" they exclaimed.

"Ch'ang-an moon, same-same," the Chinese consultant said, giving the film its title.

A tall bald man wearing Chinese clothes sits on the floor, writing with a brush.

A messenger hands him a scroll. He reads the poems of his friend, Yüan Chên.

Po rolls up his poem and sends it to Yüan Chên.

They could show him eating, sleeping, drinking, walking in the mountains, standing on a bridge, and riding in a boat, a coach, and on horseback.

They had beautiful stock footage, including scenes of battle.

Po's poem "The Hat Given to the Poet by Li Chien" would be sung by Bill Monroe and the Bluegrass Boys:

> *Long ago a white-haired gentleman*
> *You made the present of a black gauze hat.*
> *The gauze hat still sits on my head;*
> *But you already are gone to the Nether Springs.*
> *The thing is old, but still fit to wear;*
> *The man is gone and will never be seen again.*
> *Out on the hill the moon is shining to-night*
> *And the trees on your tomb are swayed by the*
> *autumn wind.*

LITTLE FRIEDA Lorraine rides in a carriage pushed by Margie.

Margie wears a Claire McCardell popover dress with an adjustable waist.

She is taking Frieda to see Grandmother Lorraine, who says mean things about Margie's weight.

Margie talks back. "You criticize Jane's hair, and she's been on seven *Harper's Bazaar* covers!"

"Don't be like this girl," Loretta says to little Frieda and laughs her merry laugh.

CAROLE'S HUSBAND, Jake, was always at the studio, and she was lonely in their mansion.

One day while Carole was out shopping she saw a tearoom where fortunes were told.

She took off her rings and went in.

While drinking her tea she noticed some things for sale.

The reader said she would marry a powerful man and live in a big house.

"Is there anything you want to ask?"

"No, thank you."

Carole chose a crystal ball, paid her check, and went out to the street.

She put on her rings and took the crystal ball out of its bag and looked into it.

She saw a woman standing under a palm tree.

"Run!" Carole told her, a moment before an earthquake shook Santa Barbara.

"*Madre de Dios*," the woman cried, wild-eyed, "an angel saved me from that tree!"

A MAN was backing a car uphill through an intersection.

He felt Carole's hand on his shoulder and heard her say, "What are you doing?"

THE STORIES of the woman and the palm tree and the man in the car were in the *Examiner* the next morning.

Carole went out to buy a scrapbook. On her way to the shops she had some fun.

A man had stabbed his wife and was going to throw the knife in the river.

"Don't do that," Carole said.

He ran all over the place, not knowing where to hide the bloody knife.

Everywhere he tried—under a rock, in a hole in a tree—Carole said, "Don't put it there!"

The river was the Rio Grande, and the police were Texas Rangers.

AN ANGEL STAYED MY HAND, said the *Examiner* the following morning.

Dateline—Rio Grande City, Texas.

"DARLING," CAROLE said to Jake at breakfast, "I love these Earth Angel stories."

"Do you, darling?"

"Yes, and I'd like to have a clipping service so I don't miss any of them."

"I'll tell Miss List to arrange it."

He kissed her and left.

CAROLE WENT over to Jane's, where she met the original owner of some of Jane's clothes.

She was the first ghost Carole had ever seen.

Noli Long, the editor-in-chief of *Harper's Bazaar*, had sent Jane a carton of Fox-Brownies from their New York office.

Their former owner, Mrs. Smullyan, came with them. She lived with Jane and Cesar and knew Margie and Faidoh, but they had never seen her.

"What is your name?" asked Carole.

"Mrs. Smullyan."

She liked Jane very much. She was so pretty. And California was heaven.

Mrs. Smullyan was dim but grew brighter as Carole questioned her.

It fascinated Carole that both life on earth and the afterlife were really a matter of focus.

"There are lots of things I could do," Mrs. Smullyan said, "but I don't know how. I never was good at instructions.

"My husband should have waited for me. He knows I have no sense of direction.

"I could go to heaven or the past or the future, but I'm afraid of my own shadow. So I stay with my clothes.

"Nobody sees me except you and Chewy. He was great in *Love and Dust*. He's a real actor."

You can have it.

Carole heard Chewy's thought and laughed so hard she had to sit down.

"Jane got Chewy because of me," Carole said. "My husband wanted to star her in a movie.

"I didn't really know him then, but I told him she wanted a dog and Jake and I fell in love."

"I wish I had done things like that," said the ghost.

"HALLO, MUMMY," said Carole. "Would you like to go out with me?"

"No, darling, I'm too tired."

Carole's mother, Ada, lived in a guesthouse on the property.

She had her own cook and maid, so she was quite independent, as she liked to say.

Hot dishes steamed on the sideboard.

Like many a heroine, Ada loved playing Solitaire.

Every layout had a different atmosphere, and there was a joke she never tired of: she'd get a ten, a nine—and instead of an eight, there'd be an Ace.

Jake kept her supplied with new decks of cards.

This morning, Ada, wearing a cashmere robe over her nightgown, was reading the paper while drinking a cup of tea.

It was open to the Earth Angel story.

"I know she's you," she said to Carole.

In the latest story, a screenwriter was driving home drunk when the angel made him swerve into a bush.

Then she said, "Sweet dreams," sort of sarcastically.

"You have the gift."

"How do you know?"

"You got it from me."

"Mummy, do you know any ghosts?"

"Stay away from them, darling. They're bores because they're totally self-absorbed."

"That's true of Mrs. Smullyan."

"When did she die?"

"Ten years ago, I'd say."

"She needs an *ami de voyage*.

"Being dead is rather complicated. There are a great many things one can do."

"She knows that."

"Yes, but she must do something! Eventually their lights go out. Traveling in space isn't that hard. Children do it. Oops. Sorry, darling."

"I do want to help her. Even if she's a bit of a bore, she has been very kind. She said my baby changed her mind about coming."

"Yes." Her mother smiled at her. "That was kind, and I'm sure it's true. I do want to help you. Look in the obituaries. Find some gent to assist her.

"Appeal to his chivalry.

"And the next time you see a ghost, ignore it. They don't know you're psychic."

SAME CH'ANG-AN Moon would start filming soon, but the writers were stuck. The boss at Paramount kept saying something was missing.

Someone came up with the idea of a librarian who loved Po Chü-i and wished she knew him.

They would have a chaste romance across the centuries, like *The Ghost and Mrs. Muir.*

NOW THAT Mrs. Smullyan knew Carole, she was starting to get around L.A.

Carole was looking at clothes at an exclusive shop when the ghost appeared.

The ghost looked through the racks, making exclamations of disgust.

She removed garments from the racks and held them up to see them. It looked like Carole was throwing them!

"Sit down, Mrs. Hirsh," the saleslady said, handing her a glass of water.

Mrs. Smullyan took the other chair and said, "My daughter couldn't wait to clean out my house and sell it.

"She packed my Fox-Brownie dresses and gave them to Mrs. Long at *Harper's*.

"I was standing right there when she said mean things about my house.

"I was active in charitable organizations. We put on fashion shows to raise money."

Carole thanked the saleslady and went to lunch.

The ghost stole bits of food from Carole's plate and left them on the table.

Carole reminded herself to check the obituaries.

"YOU READ my mind, Mr. Hirsh!"

Across town from Carole and Mrs. Smullyan's restaurant, the jeweler put a piece of black velvet on the counter and set a kneeling yellow camel on it.

"Look at this jade. Pick it up. See how warm and mellow it is."

"I thought jade was green."

"You joke. There are five colors: white, yellow, black, red, and green.

"White and yellow are the best. The fine carving makes it more precious.

"You can't carve jade with a knife. You have to use a stick and an abrasive.

"They say when you touch fine jade, it feels like an unearthly stream."

"I'll take it, and I want something for my wife."

The jeweler showed him twin brooches set with diamonds and sapphires.

"There's a lady in Paris who wears two of everything. The others copy her."

"It's good for you," Jake said, writing out a check.

"HOW ARE my two girls?" Jake asked, putting the packages on the dinner table.

As Ada watched her daughter pin the brooches on either side of her sweater, she wondered if Jake knew they were having twins.

PARAMOUNT CAST Betty Pringle as the librarian who falls in love with Po Chü-i.

She was never in his world.

He appeared at her library.

CESAR WAS kneeling in his yard.

"What are you doing?" asked Margie.

"Planting bamboo."

"That's nice."

She never knew what to say to him. She was afraid he would read Po's poem about eating bamboo shoots to her.

THE L.A.P.D. was falling apart.

Chief Conger said, "We need you back, Margie." They were getting bad press.

"You ran the department better than me.

"I'll give you a raise."

Margie went back to work and now, every afternoon, Faidoh walked to Loretta's, pushing Frieda in her carriage.

Lately, Loretta was never home.

FAIDOH GOT a letter from Singapore.

His mother was living in a British community. It reminded her of the song "Far Away Places," she said.

Was he sure Margie was the right girl for him?

She had gone there with her friend Mr. Fairfield who was getting a divorce. Loretta was sure they'd be married soon.

She was sending a little pair of silk shoes for Frieda.

AT THE premiere of *Same Ch'ang-an Moon*, Jane looked enchanting in a Fox-Brownie dress of white European silk printed with gray and black locomotives.

They were driven by women engineers in striped caps and bib overalls.

Her gloves matched the dress.

The former owner of the dress, Mrs. Smullyan, was there, too.

As she mingled with the guests, she bumped into several old acquaintances.

"Well hello," she said. "Fancy meeting you here! What brings you to L.A.?"

They couldn't see or hear her. They swatted themselves where she touched them.

Faidoh and Margie had invited Detective Works. He knew all the stars.

The stars tried to think of his name, listing the detective shows on TV.

"No, no. He's a real detective," the woman sitting next to Greta Peck said.

"Did you know Cesar wanted Paramount to cast Erna Laing as the girl?"

"She's as old as the hills!"

Works turned and frowned at the women.

Miss Laing was in her forties.

She and her rancher husband had come from Oklahoma for the premiere.

The lights dimmed, everyone settled down, and what followed was pure magic.

The poems Cesar wrote with brush and ink had been made by a Chinese calligrapher.

When Betty sang, "Youth believes in love and beauty," and Cesar answered, "But how long can they last?" the audience spontaneously applauded.

They loved the high lonesome sound of Bill Monroe and the Bluegrass Boys.

As they left for the party, they looked up at the moon and thought, "It's the same one!"

AS CAROLE and her mother left the premiere, a beaming woman cried, "Alice!" and barreled toward them.

"Blast," thought Ada Camell. "Why did I let Carole talk me into coming out with her?" She recognized the woman at once.

The woman turned to a friend. "I don't believe it! It's my old friend, Alice Corgi!"

"Hello, Tumpy," Ada said. "May I present my daughter, Carole?"

"How do you do?"

Carole thought, "Alice?"

"Well, what an absurdly splendid surprise! Aren't we all a long way from home!"

Jenny's Birthday

QUEEN OF ENGLAND'S COUSINS ARE ALIVE

HOLLYWOOD—Cousins of Queen Elizabeth II believed killed in a London air raid are living here.

Lady Alice Corgi, living in Hollywood since 1943 as Miss Ada Camell, had a memory loss, she says.

"Mummy, we live in Kensington Palace," the six-year-old Lady Carole piped.

"I didn't believe her," Lady Alice said, and they left London and eventually settled here.

Their apartment in Kensington Palace was damaged in the air raid.

Lady Alice is ninth in the line of succession to the English throne.

Her daughter, Lady Carole, a former model for *Harper's Bazaar*, is married to MGM producer Jake Hirsh.

Her Majesty, Queen Elizabeth, expressed pleasure that her cousins are alive.

"What happened, Mummy?" Carole asked when they were alone.

"Your father had a temper, as we used to say. Your Aunt Pepita had gone out with him, so I thought he was desirable.

"Then, when I had you, I realized that you were really what I wanted.

"So, one night during the Blitz, I took you and escaped.

"I made up the name Camell. I thought it would appeal to a six-year-old. And I made up the story you like, about the London bobby saying, 'Surely not the whole thing!'

"We came in a bomber that needed repair. A soldier gave you a candy bar, and you slept most of the way.

"I had lost our papers and we ended up being shuffled around until we ended up in the Aleutians of all places."

"What did you do?"

"A handsome captain in the Signal Corps was receptive to helping us.

"He had a wife and baby daughter. I can still see their picture on his desk. He was the second son in his family, so he was always for the underdog. He wrote to someone he had worked with at the Pentagon, and got it fixed."

"Where is the Captain now?"

"Back in Minnesota, I imagine, at the head of his beloved electronics company. I never saw him again.

"So here we are, now that Tumpy has spilled the beans. Your Aunt Pepita rang. My sister and her daughter, your cousin Penny, will descend on us soon. She told me that your father is dead. You'll inherit Grandison."

"What's Grandison?"

"I'd give it to the National Trust if I were you."

Lazlo Molnar was in Hollywood trying to put together a property for MGM.

One day in a bookstore he saw *Jenny's Birthday Book* by Esther Averill.

He bought it from a cloying salesgirl who kept asking about his "little ones."

Wresting the package from her, he went to a drugstore, but it was too public.

In his hotel bungalow he eagerly paged through it, sounding out the words.

I see Lazlo before me as I write. Below his black beret were black-rimmed eyeglasses, a large nose, and thin curling lips. He wore a dark scarf and a tan trench coat.

He thought Esther Averill, who had been an editor for *Women's Wear Daily* and founded a publishing house in Paris, was a primitive American genius.

He, a European, was a great genius.

The flowers would sing, the moon would sing. Jenny's kind owner, Captain Tinker, would sing.

He listed the cast:

Jenny Linsky, a shy black cat

Her brothers, Edward and Checkers

Captain Tinker

Pickles the Fire Cat

Florio (wears an Indian feather)

Two big fighters, Sinbad and The Duke = Rocky (Gene Kelly)

A little stranger (female)

Jane Lorraine accepted the role of Jenny Linsky. Cesar, no longer under contract to Paramount Pictures, signed up to play Captain Tinker.

AT THE guesthouse on Jake Hirsh's estate, Carole was having so much fun.

First she learned her mother, Ada Camell, was actually Lady Alice Corgi. Now her aunt, Lady Pepita Airedale, and cousin, Lady Penny Airdale, had popped by on their way to China.

"Pepita!" her mother had cried. "You don't look a day over thirty!"

"Oh goodie! I'm Penny! You must be my Auntie Alice."

"Of course, she's Alice," Pepita said. "You sly minx! We were worried off our heads. Here, I brought you Gran's pearls."

"Could I have some of that food?" Penny pulled up a chair. "It's lovely."

"I don't think I've had this before. What is it?"

"Fried matzos," said Alice.

"Delicious! Well, we must dash. Off to China."

"I want to communicate with Mummy's spirit," Pepita said. "She died in the Blitz, you know."

"Yes, I'm sorry," Alice said.

"And here are the papers and keys to Coverly. Just when I couldn't think what to do with that place or Gran's pearls," Pepita said, "you turned up alive."

"What's Coverly?" asked Carole.

"Oh, I expect Aunt Alice will tell you all about it! Nicer than Grandison any day. So good to meet you, cousin Carole! I've organized a cave on Hua mountain. I expect I'll get eaten by a tiger."

Pepita smiled fondly at Penny and said to Carole, "She's why they call us eccentric."

"Pepita, wait," Alice said. "Will you do me a favor please? It's about a ghost."

CHEWY RAISED his head. Mrs. Smullyan had a visitor!

"Come along," Pepita urged. "You can come back whenever you like."

"I won't know how," Mrs. Smullyan said.

"If you stay, you'll fizzle. Come on, it's a lovely journey and great fun."

"How would I fizzle?"

"Stay and see."

"Wait, I'm coming! Goodbye, Chewy."

He felt her hand on his coat.

He never knew how she fit in. She was a ghost from New York.

SECRECY SURROUNDED *Jenny's Birthday.*

The scenes were painted in the flat primary and secondary colors of Esther Averill's illustrations.

Props were copied and constructed.

Lazlo sneered at the idea of his cast wearing ears and tails.

Gene Kelly wore a white T-shirt, black chinos, white socks, and black loafers.

Tab Hunter's Pickles wore a yellow shirt, khakis, white socks, and black loafers.

Jane wore a black leotard, a red neckerchief, and black ballerina slippers.

Jay Silverheels as Florio wore buckskins like the ones he had worn with the Lone Ranger, despite a threatened lawsuit from the Wrather Corporation.

"Americans are children. They will love it," thought Lazlo.

I think he was surprised by its beauty.

The cast and crew knew they were filming a classic, and so it has proved to be.

CESAR WAS offered his new contract early and he refused. He told the studio his next film would be his last.

Government was considered an art in ancient China, and Po Chü-i was a censor.

"If Your Majesty's political measures should be at variance with The Way, would Your Majesty not be eager to know about it?" he wrote in one of his memorials.

The Journey to Washington, with Cesar as Abraham Lincoln, was a logical follow-up. It famously begins with the Farewell Address at Springfield, Illinois:

> *My friends—No one, not in my situation, can appre-*
> *ciate my feeling of sadness at this parting. I now leave,*
> *not knowing when, or whether ever, I may return, with a*
> *task before me greater than that which rested upon Wash-*

ington. Without the assistance of that Divine Being, who ever attended him, I cannot succeed. With that assistance I cannot fail. Trusting in Him, who can go with me, and remain with you and be everywhere for good, let us confidently hope that all will yet be well.

Paramount made the film to try to win him back, but Cesar had decided. He was going back to the hut on his mountain.

JANE LORRAINE never married, never tried to look young (she turned seventy this year), and never stopped working. Her latest film is *Little Lady Eat No Candy* with Ray Ng and John Travolta.

The plot is great fun. John Travolta tries to kill Jane to prevent her from revealing his past. She doesn't know him, and Ray Ng has to protect her. As one reviewer said, "She doesn't act but lets the part come through her."

Jane has always had a German shepherd since her beloved Chü-i. He was followed by Chü-ar, Chü-san, Chü-syh, and Chü-wu. Her sixth will be Chü-lio.

Jake and Carole Hirsh had twins, a boy and girl. Birdie and Hugh now live in Coverly and Grandison, the English estates they inherited.

Faidoh Lorraine made only one movie. He was cast in *GI Cowboy* at the suggestion of his father. Faidoh played the guitar and sang in the barracks, but his part was cut after a week of filming. Rumor has it he had a halo that appeared on film.

Faidoh and Margie now have grandchildren and still live in Dorey Deane's old bungalow. Their daughter, Frieda, is reportedly a frequent guest at Coverly, the home of her cousin, Birdie Hirsh.

Most of the family attended last year's annual village jumble sale. They went to every booth and bought homemade jams, cakes, and dishcloths.

Wearing a chiffon dress and an amusing hat, Jane gave a charming speech and was presented with a bouquet and a china dog.

APPENDIX: SELECTIONS FROM BIRDIE A. HIRSH'S DIARY

1964

God keeps us in heaven until he puts us in a story. Then he puts us on earth.

We pray we are in a good story.

Johanna Spyri made Karla walk again. Did Karla pray to Johanna Spyri?

Did Johanna Spyri pray to God to let her write a good story?

"YOU ARE gathering your characters delightfully," Jane Austen wrote to a niece who was writing a novel.

Frieda and I think we are delightful characters.

We have an Aunt Jane, but she would never write to us.

FRIEDA AND I are Jewish! We went to Sunday School and heard the story of Adam and Eve and the snake.

I passed Frieda a note: "God is gathering His characters delightfully."

We are people of the book! We have a prayer, "Who is like unto Thee, Almighty God, Author of life and death, source of salvation?"

Frieda is Jewish because her mother is Jewish. My father's mother was Jewish.

We don't know if I am really Jewish or if Hugh is a lord, even though he will inherit Grandison.

I will get Coverly. Frieda and I are planning our debutante ball there.

My grandmother is related to the Queen, so I can be introduced to her, and Frieda's grandfather is Cesar Lorraine, so the Queen will also want to meet her.

We'll have a brilliant season and be proposed to by two lords, but there the dream ends.

We are proud Americans, delightful characters, and Californians. We would never be like that idiot Isabel Archer in the novel by Henry James.

I made up a girl called Cricket but couldn't think of anything for her to do.

1965

MOM HAS been in England, and Dad and I came to meet her.

We went to Yom Kippur services at Temple Emanu-El, on Fifth Avenue.

At home everyone rises for the Mourner's Kaddish.

Here Dad and I stood alone to hear my grandmother's name, Birdie Birnbaum Hirsh.

I also thought of Cricket.

I want to go to Hebrew Union College and be a rabbi. Frieda, with her beautiful voice, can be a cantor.

"The departed whom we now remember have entered into the peace of life eternal. They still live on earth in the acts of goodness they performed and in the hearts of those who cherish their memory. May the beauty of their life abide among us as a loving benediction.

"May the Father of peace send peace to all who mourn, and comfort all the bereaved among us."

Dad and I sat down. The man on my other side said, "I'm sorry for your trouble. I'm Billy Rose."

Lady Tannenbaum and Myself

to David
with love

Our cat Pluche
is my
writing master,
whenever I have a
thought he bangs
his food dish
until I forget it.

If the Lorraines hadn't moved to Hollywood, I probably wouldn't exist.

My parents met because my father wanted to star Jane Lorraine in a movie.

I read this in *The Lorraines in Hollywood*, a novel that quotes my childhood diaries.

The author, M. B. Goffstein, said she bought them at a rummage sale in Westchester County. As Miss Goffstein neared the end of the book, she made her selections and typed them in.

When I rang Miss Goffstein, she was excited. I heard her say to her husband, "It's Birdie Hirsh!"

"I'm sorry. Who?"

Her husband didn't remember me, though Brooke says it is her best book.

The first thing Miss Goffstein wanted to know was whether I was a rabbi.

You should have heard her laugh when I said I was Lady Tannenbaum.

"Did Frieda marry a lord, too?"

"She's Orthodox and has six children."

"What!" she shouted. "Are they cute?"

"They're in their twenties."

"Their twenties!"

She certainly loves to talk.

I HEARD Miss Goffstein paging through her book. "Have you heard from Lady Penny?"

I debated whether to say she'd been eaten by a tiger and hear her scream.

I think her husband, who seems very quiet, was pleased she had a phone pal.

"I'll put Brooke on the wire," he would say, after we'd said hello.

WHEN BROOKE said she found my old diaries at a rummage sale, I wondered if I had hidden them in a desk or bureau that my mother gave away.

It reminded me of *The Chest with a Secret* by Yvonne de Bremond d'Ars.

I mentally walked through my parents' home on the beach in Santa Monica.

Then I called my mother.

Mummy and I often speak several times a day, and now that I have Brooke, I'm lucky to get off the phone.

"Of course I remember them, darling. I put them in a carton and mailed them to you.

"Didn't you get them?"

California air and sunshine and fresh fruit and vegetables keep my parents slim and strong.

At eighty, Jake is the image of a Hollywood producer married to a tall, elegant blond.

He is fifteen years older than Carole but doesn't look it.

I had no ambition and was glad to marry their friend Morrie, who is Carole's age.

I APPEAR at the end of *The Lorraines in Hollywood* because Brooke likes young artists.

Now I feel I have to fulfill my early promise (and all the writing tips Brooke has been giving me), so I am taking notes for a book called *Conversations with an Author*.

"BE SURE you see a scene and hear the words before you write it. Don't make it up.

"For writing's a PLEH-sure, and rewriting is grief—but a false-hearted SEN-tence, is worse than a thief," Brooke sang to the tune of "On Top of Old Smokey."

We were getting to be quite good friends.

She said, "I've had the best life!

"When my father was in the Aleutians in World War II, Sir Thomas Beecham used to wait near the elevators and carry me around the hotel lobby in Seattle.

"In grade school the girls said my father was as handsome as a movie star.

"My first husband was a student of Mme. Lhevinne. I attended her master classes.

"'Come to me, come to me,' she would say, her hands stroking the keys.

"She meant don't play *on* the piano, play *from* the piano. I have followed her advice in drawing and writing.

"Mme. Freschl played trios with Albert Einstein and the King of Norway.

"She said, 'Einshtein, count!'

"'I wish he could have met you, he would have *loffed* you,' she told me."

"Those are blessings, aren't they?"

"Yes!"

"I'm extremely grateful people like my books, but I never bought into it.

"I even changed my name as an author once. That was a mistake.

"I say I stopped drawing because my eyesight isn't as good, but it's still very good.

"I stopped because I wanted to try other things.

"Drawing is a tool. It's a way to discover things and work out problems.

"I love writing fiction now. It isn't as scary as drawing, and you are never lonely."

I thought it was so cute the way Brooke was eager to tell what she knew.

When I'm her age, I expect I'll be the same, should anyone who is writing a biography of my father, Jake Hirsh, or a history of Coverly seek me out.

BROOKE SAID, "There is one scary thing. I'm running out of notebooks! I had a lot of one kind, spiral-bound with a dachshund on the cover.

"I bought eleven of them.

"I've almost finished the tenth. It's bad to be old and out of notebooks.

"David found them for me on the internet, but now they have a cat on the cover.

"I hope it's a Rex," I said.

"Do you still have any of the notebooks you used?" Brooke asked. "Wait, I took out the scene where you got them."

Brooke kept discarded sections of *The Lorraines in Hollywood* on her computer.

After locating them, she read:

> Carole and her mother went up and down the creaky wooden
> aisles of the dime store collecting amusing things and
> breathing the aromas.
> They chose lilac nail polish for Birdie.
> They found her looking at a stack of blank books called
> Record Books.
> They had pebbly black paper covers, maroon cloth spines, and
> blue-lined pages.
> "Get them all," Carole said.

YOU MIGHT think I had enough on my plate, trying to keep up with the repairs on Coverly, to take on the writing of *Conversations with an Author*.

You have seen the owners of old English estates on the HG channel.

The husband collects old slate to repair the roof, the wife washes windows, and their sons ride bicycles through the drawing room and entrance hall.

My husband got his baronetcy by making scads of money, so don't look for me in a tearoom or gift shop.

In fact, stay off our grounds unless you are a friend of ours or work here.

When anything breaks, we replace it with something new and special.

We have attics filled with old furniture, some from the days of Sir Roger de Coverly.

Labels tied to them have diagrams showing where they were situated.

Like Brooke, we order from the Design Within Reach catalog.

You can't get more wonderful furniture, and there is nothing snob about it.

Have you ever spent a night sleeping on a Sonno mattress? It's just great!

Perhaps Design Within Reach will put my book in their catalog if I keep it short so this stands out.

I THOUGHT that might make a good ending for this book but was surprised to see I only have a few pages.

BROOKE SAID when she got the Design Within Reach catalog, she felt honored.

She thought they sent it because she taught at Parsons School of Design.

Her first purchase was the George Nelson bench, which we have, too.

Ours is in the entrance hall, perfect for setting things down on and dealing with boots.

The catalog cover showed an artist sitting on the bench, looking at one of his paintings, or so Brooke thought.

I got an email from Brooke showing her Vega sofa with a white canvas slipcover.

"Who's the kitty?" I asked.

"That's Pluche. He's named for the book by Jean Dutourd. Isn't the slipcover great?

"Of course he's the reason we have one. The ottoman has a slipcover, too."

I got another email with an attachment.

"That's our linen press," said Brooke. "Our walls are white. That blue is the morning light."

"Did you just get a camera?" I asked.

"No, I've had it for two and a half years. I just learned how to press the button. I was pressing it too hard."

I FELT my cell phone vibrate.

"The cat notebook came."

"Do you like it?"

"That cat could never help me write."

"I HAD an idea about Cesar," I said to Brooke. "He could do one-man shows, reading Po Chü-i's poems. It's what he loves to do anyway."

"Yes!" Brooke exclaimed. "My friend Margery loved the poems in *The Lorraines in Hollywood*.

"Another friend read a draft and said she liked the way the pages were stapled."

Brooke is certainly laconic.

MY WORK on *Conversations with an Author* has inspired me to go further.

At an auction while visiting London, Mummy won Lot 24, Hagenauer sculptures, two black cats.

At lunch, she said, "Choose one."

I was excited about one stamped "Rena, Made in Austria."

When I got home, I checked my copy of *The Lorraines in Hollywood*. And oh-ho! A character in Dorey Deane's fiction series collected bronze Hagenauer cat figurines from Rena Rosenfeld's shop. And I had one with her touchmark!

From the internet I soon learned that Rena Rosenfeld had a shop in the Waldorf in the 1940s and '50s.

She sold sculptures by Hagenauer, Baller and Bosse, some of which she might have designed.

I took out some of our stationery and began to write.

HOURS LATER, my dogs stared at me. They had never seen me act this way before.

I let them out in the backyard and returned to my desk, feeling guilty.

My mother-in-law isn't strong enough to walk them, and Morrie isn't home.

THAT EVENING, I was so excited, I called Brooke.

"The characters just appeared!" I said.

"That's wonderful!"

"I don't have a plot. So far, it's only a series of sketches.

"I even know what the people look like!"

"Isn't writing wonderful?" Brooke cried. "You solve all kinds of mysteries.

"I can't explain it—not that anyone cares. 'I have to go,'" she said, imitating her friends on the phone.

I reminded Brooke I didn't have a plot yet.

"You have to work," she said.

"MUMMY, WRITING is a marvelous experience. It's like being out in space! You have these insights—"

"I have to go. Talk to you later, darling."

I TOLD Jake about what I'd written so far.

"Where's the love interest?"

I think it's in owning a shop.

I still only have sketches. I'm not sure if it will end up as a screenplay, a musical, or a comic strip. Here's one sketch:

SYLVIA lives at the Waldorf and relaxes in her room:

SYLVIA

I want everything Rena touches.

That's why I bought these two lounge chairs.

The porter brought them up and took away the hotel
    chairs.

Now my room looks so happy!

I love being a bachelor girl.

I never think about my two divorces.

[SITS ON LOUNGE CHAIR]

But I don't know what I'd do without Rena.

THE ONLY obstacle to creating a comic strip is that I can't draw.

I sat down and drew capsule people. They came out well!

I drew show business producers in the lobby with their cigars.

Mrs. Suarez has heart-shaped lips and a chunky fur coat, and Mr. Suarez has a black hat. An excited dog pulls his lead. A librarian faints in the lobby.

"HA, HA, ha," laughed Morrie later.

I went to see what had brought this on.

He was reading *Rena's Shop at the Waldorf*.

That was intoxicating. I can see why writing can be addictive.

I kept going but hit a big snarl.

Brooke was thrilled I was having a hard time.

"You have to fight!" she said.

"It's a lot of work," I said.

"I know! You can't do anything else. You can't even go out!" she gloated.

I DECIDED *Rena's Shop at the Waldorf* wanted to be a musical.

I wrote an opening scene and showed it to Jake. He said it needed more dancers.

"TAKE IT easy," Brooke cautioned. "Don't write a lot of junk you'll have to take out."

She quoted from her book, *A Writer*,

> . . . *a writer always studies, looks, and listens.*
> *Thoughts that grow strongly*
> *in her heart*
> *and weather every mood and change of mind*
> *she will care for.*

BROOKE TAUGHT writing and illustrating at Parsons School of Design for eleven years.

She loved it. She saw her students as works of art and cared that they were authentic.

She could tell when their work was false and help them find their real work.

I took Brooke's advice to let *Rena* rest and thought to catch up on my reading. On page 91 of *Intimate Strangers: The Culture of Celebrity in America* by Richard Schickel, I read:

> *It is conventional not to waste too much sympathy on producers, and it is a convention that is always easy to honor, though it ought to be recorded that among these vulgar buccaneers there were men of shrewdness, energy and, in their way, vision.*

I felt I could no longer wait for someone to write my father, Jake Hirsh's, biography and would do it myself.

I called the author of *The Lorraines in Hollywood*.

"Hi," I said. "It's Birdie."

She was happy to hear from me. She listened to my complaint and read aloud something she said was the most beautiful thing written about artists.

It was the beginning of the introduction by W. R. Valentiner, Director of the Detroit Institute of Arts to *Letters of John B. Flannagan*.

> *The letters in this volume are from the hand of one of the few outstanding American born sculptors of our time, John B. Flannagan, whom a tragic fate has taken from us at an early age. If we remember how easy a life, compared to his, many artists of less originality have had in our day, we feel what history has shown so often, that no one is able to judge the value of an artist rightly before his death.*

> *It is as if nature wants to blind us so that the great work can be borne in the silence of the night, without being disturbed in the suffering hour by a criticizing crowd.*

"I was struck by that," Brooke said, "because I wrote about Van Gogh,"

> *but was his misery like dust,*
> *purposely kicked up*
> *to keep all jealous eyes*
> *from his brushstrokes of whirling beauty?*

"Are you saying my father is an artist?"

"He had the vision to star Jane Lorraine in *Love and Dust*, and he invited Lazlo Molnar to Hollywood.

"Lazlo did nothing for years. Then suddenly he wrote and directed *Jenny*!

"Jake is an artist, and people are his medium.

"His actors and directors remind me of a picture book of mine called *Artists' Helpers Enjoy the Evenings*.

"The artists' helpers are pastel sticks who wear berets.

"I wrote it because David [her husband] loved the idea that when daylight failed in the artists' studios and they could no longer work, they went to cafés.

"Your father's way of life is the opposite of miserable, but it keeps people away.

"His beautiful suits and shoes make them feel abashed."

I wondered if Brooke felt that way about me because we are rich and have titles.

I don't wear beautiful clothes, however, as my married last name says it all regarding my figure.

"So why are you interested in John Flannagan?" I asked.

"I think I own two of his sculptures."

So she was rich! I figured they cost a fortune.

But she had bought one at a thrift shop and the other at a consignment shop.

"But they're problematical," she said. "Here, I'll email you pictures."

"I got them," I said.

The marble fish was signed "John A. Flanagan," with one *n*, and he was John B. Flannagan, with two *n*'s.

I was disappointed, but Brooke said the *F* was made the way Flannagan made his *F*'s as far as she could tell, from a fuzzy little reproduction of a drawing in a book.

"He used the initial B because there was an earlier sculptor named John Flanagan (with one *n*)."

"Ah," I said.

"But the earlier John Flanagan was more classical. He designed the quarter."

"The coin? Love his work."

"Me too! Anyway, our John B. Flannagan was incarcerated in Bloomingdale's."

"Bloomingdale's?"

"The Bloomingdale Insane Asylum, down in White Plains. Not from here in Westchester.

"He was allowed to work, but not too much. He had a problem with work. I'll read you this from the time before the asylum," she said.

> *At times he worked with tremendous speed, producing almost daily a small piece of sculpture, but as he knew no relaxation—he was not interested in sports and disliked moving pictures as inartistic—he sought to obliterate his exhaustion by drinking.*

"He might have been so drunk and rattled he forgot his name as he scratched it in the marble.

"Or someone named John A. Flanagan carved it.

"Or he might have been in the insane asylum when he did it."

Brooke certainly has a romantic spirit about art she finds at thrift shops.

The other sculpture, the granite bird, wasn't signed but was attached to a stone that had the initials "WB" carved in it.

Brooke, who sees crime everywhere, thought WB pretended to have carved it and take credit for a Flannagan.

"I spent a fortune on old books about his work but his life was so tragic, it's depressing reading about him. He got hit by cars twice, because he was drunk.

"He should have been a bartender and made an honest living. He could have carved in the mornings.

"He said, 'Someday the bandwagon will beat a noisy path to my door.'

"No one has even heard of him.

"He finally couldn't stand it anymore and killed himself.

"Anyway, these sculptures aren't in the books, and I can't reach Robert Joseph Forsyth, who wrote his PhD thesis on Flannagan.

"He isn't where he was, at the University of Colorado.

"Forsyth was doing a *catalogue raisonné* but gave his materials to the Smithsonian. David said, he packed it in.

"So I think," Brooke concluded, "I'll just put the stone bird outside under our American beech. Flannagan wanted his sculptures to be outside and I love it. Even if it isn't his."

I rightly reckoned the way to get off the topic of sad Mr. Flannagan was to ask about her.

"Did you want to be a sculptor?" I asked Brooke.

"I would have loved to, but I couldn't afford a studio and I had to make a living.

"My picture books were like solo shows, and I got to keep the originals.

"I carved a log at Bennington, and then I carved four little figures that I photographed in four books."

I DIDN'T really want to write a biography of my father, I just wanted to be up and doing something while giving *Rena* a rest.

I went in to London thinking I would have a look in some galleries and ask about Flannagan.

I felt the first person I met would tell me there were two missing Flannagans, a bird and a fish.

Brooke would be rich!

I think I may be spending too much time talking to her. I am starting to think like her as well.

No luck in London.

Back home, I sent Brooke an email with what I had so far for *Rena*.

RENA is in her shop opening an order, even though she has customers.

MRS. PRESTON lives at the Waldorf. She buys herself things from Rena and has them wrapped and sent to her room.

She has her hair done in the hotel, buys her clothes there, orders dinner in her suite, and opens her purchases, imitating Rena.

She rips off the paper and admires what she has bought, but she can't sleep.

Putting her mink on over her nightgown, she goes down to the lobby.

Standing in front of Rena's shuttered shop, she sings:

MRS. PRESTON
(singing)
Where does Rena go at night
To a box in the Bronx with a sick aunt
Or a lovely apartment on Park Avenue
With nicer things than she shows me and you

THE SUAREZES come in the Lexington Avenue entrance, wearing evening clothes.

They are sympathetic and good-naturedly try their English:

THE SUAREZES
(singing)
What does Rena do at night
Her shop is empty

The little objects are undisciplined
They do things they shouldn't

A MAN enters from Lexington, walking a DACHSHUND.
It is unclear if he and his dog live at the Waldorf or if
they buy the evening paper there as part of their evening
walk.
The MAN learns the song from MRS. PRESTON
and MR. AND MRS. SUAREZ and dances with them,
holding his little DOG.
He sings:

MAN
(singing)
What does Rena do at night
In her apartment on Lex
She gives dinners for friends
Who bring her flowers

A BELLBOY sings:

BELLBOY
(singing)
I think Rena is kept by a man
He wants her to keep busy
While he is with his family
So he financed the shop
The five new friends say goodnight.

MRS. PRESTON, looking happy, takes the elevator to
her suite.

The SUAREZES go to the bar for a nightcap, and the
MAN and DACHSHUND go to the newsstand.

As MAIDS and BELLBOYS *clean the lobby, emptying ashtrays and stamping designs in the white sand,* RENA *opens her shop.*

The bookshop, the beauty shop, the jewelry shop, and the clothes shop on the Lexington Avenue side come to life as RENA *sings:*

RENA
(singing)
There is always something going on
In my shop
Look at these rhinoceroses
carved from Mushakashula wood.
A person who looks rich
May spend a dollar
Someone who looks poor
May spend hundreds

MRS. PRESTON *steps off the elevator and sees the* SUAREZES, *who ask how she slept.*

MRS. PRESTON
I had a wonderful dream. I dreamed I had a
shop called Just a Few Little Things.

MY CELL phone vibrated.

"This is wonderful!" Brooke was delighted.

"This is the best present I could have," she said.

She would be sixty-seven the next day.

I thought she was a little over the top.

"No," she said. "Mrs. Preston was floating in space and you found her!

"Now you are telling her story, repairing the world, making things right."

"Jake says it should be Rena! with an exclamation mark."

THE NEXT day, for her sixty-seventh birthday, I gave Brooke a nice surprise.

"Penny," I said at tea, dialing a number on my phone, "let's call the author of *The Lorraines in Hollywood*."

"What larks!" Penny said.

"Tell Brooke about your trip home from China through Afghanistan."

"Hello?" Brooke answered.

"Brookie! It's Birdie! Hold the wire," I said like David, her husband, and handed the phone to Penny.

After they introduced themselves and Brooke stopped exclaiming her delight, Penny told her story.

"Well, you see, I went down Hua mountain to get cigarettes and couldn't find my way back.

"'Huashan?' I asked the farmers.

"They kept pointing west.

"After I had walked a very long time, the people started to look different.

"A tribal leader showed me a picture of Abraham Lincoln, and I tapped my chest.

"They thought I meant I was related to him, and they treated me with great kindness.

"I gave them a little keepsake from home, and they escorted me to Kabul.

"It was filled with English and American soldiers.

"They wanted me out of there, and I didn't have to use my Barclay's card."

"She was gone for forty years," I said so Brooke could hear.

"I was lucky I had a shawl I wore over my head, because it was so damn cold," Penny said.

"Hi, it's Birdie again," I said, taking back the phone. "Happy birthday, Brookie. Has it been a good day?"

"The best," she said. "I bought a lead dachshund from the 1930s."

PENNY IS visiting just in time for another jumble. Horrors. Home-made jams, cakes, and dishcloths, ho!

More family was arriving.

"Hide the silver," I told Morrie. I had seen Hugh's car coming up the drive.

I kissed his wife, Pam, and she sank down on a sofa saying, "This is so luxurious!"

It was our new Vega sofa, quite low and firm, but the back cushions are soft, and it's very comfortable.

Brooke has taken in hand this book I wrote about her called *Conversations with an Author* and retitled it *Lady Tannenbaum and Myself*.

For myself, I have gained some insight. It was a wonderful feeling to create something.

Mario's Garage

"THIS IS VOMG,
    the Voice of Mario's Garage.
Think of Mario's when you see the light,
just a short, friendly stop on the long road to Heaven."

Burning in the dark like stars,
campfires light the road to Mario's.
Travelers swap stories in the night.

A documentary filmmaker
says to a soldier,
"Angels are like steel.
Their souls and bodies are one.
They're tall and beautiful.
You may meet one."

Friends greet lost friends.
"Bonjour, Etienne."
"Bonjour. I was eaten by a bear.
It was beautiful.
He picked me up and held me.
I felt his breath as he said a prayer of thanks."

A cat tells a professor,
"I projected myself through space to get a soul."
"We all do that. It's a known fact in botany.
The soul is above the head, the spirit is in the heart."

Brother finds brother.
"Ben. How you doing?"
"I'm out of prison."
"Have you seen Ma?"
"She don't want to know us."
"She says she wouldn't have touched money from the Mob."
"Was it bad in prison?"
"I had my light."
"To be an architect?"
"I'm going back."
"I'll go with you and help any way I can."

Around a campfire there are the souls of
books bound for Heaven.
Four Hopalong Cassidy novels by Louis L'Amour and
The Hurricane of 1938 on Eastern Long Island
by Ernest S. Clowes are trail mates and
make room for two strangers.
One of the newcomers speaks,
"The uncle, Kuang,
said to his nephew, Shou,
If one knows what's sufficient,
one will not be disgraced.
If one knows when to stop,
one will not be in danger.
When one's task has been achieved,
to retire of oneself is the way of Heaven.
If we do not go away,
I fear that we shall regret it.
That same day, uncle and nephew both

asked to resign on account of sickness.
They were granted three full months leave of absence.
Kuang then claiming that their illness was serious,
memorialized to request their release.
The Emperor granted both their request
because they were very old.
A feast was set outside the eastern city gate.
Several hundred carriages escorted them.
When the farewells were over,
they returned to their home with shrill cries."

"That's some yarn. Who are you, hombres?" Hoppy asks.
"We're Volumes 1 and 2 of T'ao Yuan-ming
translated by A. R. Davis."
"Welcome to the road, partners."

Biography of
Miss Go Chi

To David!

Banners fly above
the stalls, across
from the docks and
vast cement
terminal, saying,
Goodbye
and
*Remember
Me.*
Miss Go
eagerly
looks on
the tables.
There are
stacks of
pennies and dimes;
plastic alarm clocks
with sayings
Rise and Shine,
and *It's That Time Again*,
and *Up and At 'Em*;
and refrigerator
magnets.

My great niece
found the earrings
I sent her
at a thrift shop,
someone remarks.
Angels make
deliveries.

A boat pulls in to a slip.
Passengers disembark.
Will you give this
to my daughter,
asks a woman taking
off her ruby ring.
Put it on the
kitchen counter
so she sees it.
She is such a
ding-a-ling
which is why I
wouldn't let her
wear it.

THE air is crystal
cold and clear.
The ground is
high and white.
Miss Go Chi is
in Heaven.
Walking up
the long drive,
she realizes it's
Bennington.

Her house is the
first one you come to.
She passes the tree
that fills her room
with yellow light on
cold autumn mornings.
She enters Booth House
and climbs the stairs.

Did you have a good
Non-Resident Term?
The two Sophomores
leaning over
the banister,
Ynez and Esmeralda,
have the double next
to her single.

I had a wonderful
life,
it was like
a dream.

Her room is just
as she left it.
Her books
surprise her.
I had them
all this time,
she thinks.

Miss Go wakes up
under her quilt.

Poetry Workshop
is in The Barn
behind
Commons.
There are girls
in leotards
and dangly
earrings.
Are you taking
poetry with
Po Chü-i?
one asks.
I didn't
know he was
teaching this
semester.

HEAVEN is vast
and Bennington,
circa 1959,
is but one tiny section.

IT is
comforting
to note
that we are
only
images
projected
from afar.

Our souls
are in
the stars

so if
a comet
destroys us

we will
survive

and our
stories

will be on
the air.

THE sky is black
the stars are
mighty
as Miss Go
walks back from
North Bennington
holding a small
handful of peanuts
from the vending
machine
at the all-night
gas station.

Brooke's Last Words

Chosen from
conversations with visitors at
the Regional Hospice,
Danbury, Connecticut,
November–December 2017

You know
I've had a good life,
        a great life.
I'm going to be seventy-seven on December 20th.
I have no problem dying. None.
I mean there are people I don't want
        to leave but—
Death is my friend.
Death and hope.
Hope.

I believe in an afterlife.
But if it's not there,
I won't weep and moan, because
        I've had fun with it.
I've been writing about death
        for twenty years.
I like a fight. A good fight.
Like Jacob and the angel,
"I will not let you go except thou bless me."
Crazy,
        wonderful,
glorious.

Wrestle with what you have to be better
          and better and better.
It's the understanding that you're a genius,
          every single one of you.
And you have millions of gifts
          to choose from.
And you have to get cracking
          because you can't use all of them.
I'm not creative. Just the opposite.
There's the truth, and I'm on to it,
          and I have to uncover it.

I'm made and I made things.
We all make the truth appear.
A tree makes a leaf appear,
          that's the truth.
Makes a place for birds to sit,
          that's the truth.
(Oh God, what a wonderful time I'm having.)
There's room for you to do your work.
Listen—
We're going to tell
          such stories.

Afterword

Paper Dolls

by Doreen Stock

for Brooke Goffstein

"God lost interest in people ages ago and now is just happy with a paper doll collection," you once expressed, but no one reading these words could understand how God's happiness could ever be so bound up in this sunlight on green carpet, two cousins, all the time in the world coursing thru their child bodies, scissors, paper, colored pencils and crayons only, producing such lasting joy. You a six-year-old teacher to five-year-old me as we sat, intent, to draw the little white bodies, to design what they would wear. Most important: the dolls were children. Square feet, chubby hands, red mouths, tiny clear eyes. I don't remember a lot of giggling or fits of temper. No one was torn up or crumpled into waste. Our work was serious, as any act of love, our colors pure, our lines, true. God loved us doing it, and, a little jealous, perhaps, turned his back on even Harry S. Truman just to watch.

And so, I like to think, my brilliant cousin, that when your time came on the very winter day of your birth, God reached God's hand to lift you, bent the rainbowed light just so to garment your frail shoulders, let your sleeves blow long and loose, and clipped a final hem at your white feet. "I'm not going to give her shoes today," the voice of a child could be heard to say,

"Let her squish the grass between her toes. Let her run free . . ."

For Brooke

by Bill Zavatsky

I thought I'd call this
"Poem Beginning with a Line by Brooke."
The line was the title of her painting called
The Book Was the Angel, which appears
on her website and on the invitation
that brought us here today. It made me
think of anyone holding a book, an attitude
of prayer, folded hands, someone singing
alone or in a chorus. Among the books

lying with their wings folded (temporarily)
on my shelves and on my desk
are all of Brooke's—oh, maybe one or two
are missing or flew away to someone else's
bookshelf. Books are holy, I told myself
a long time ago. I buy them all the time
and can't give them away.

A book is holy—that made me think
of William Blake, staring into the night sky,
intoning "Little lamb, who made thee?
Dost thou know who made thee?"

and then of Brookie and Her Lamb, maybe
her sweetest book. Blake made his pictures,
just as Brooke did, and both made words.

My favorite of Brooke's is probably
Family Scrapbook. I used it
in my poetry workshop, and wrote to tell
her how much the students loved her poems,
these poems taken from everyday life—a new
pickup truck, the family singing as papa drove.
"I'm surprised," I wrote, "that none of your books
are identified as *poetry*." "I never told them,"
Brooke wrote back, almost in a whisper.
No one tells us what poetry is, but you can
find it everywhere in her work; you can
find it everywhere in your life

if you look around, if you look into
memory, where everything is moving
or standing still, waiting to be picked up,
drawn, colored, found words for—or do I
mean given words to?—or that we must be
ready to receive the words and shapes
and colors that radiate from the things
and people we knew and still know, how they
really do "speak to us," everything a mouth.

"He tries to make paint sing," Brooke said in
An Artist. Why do I feel that this
is the hardest poem I've ever written,
though somehow I don't want to stop
writing it? Brooke's *School of Names*,
where now she must be teaching again—
how to find the names of everything, or to
name things, or give them new names . . .

Do we get a new name in heaven? Do we
get to choose? "No ideas but in things,"
another favorite poet of mine wrote—
the ideas are in the things. And this
the old Chinese poets knew, the ones
Brooke loved: Po Chü-i, T'ao Yuan-ming,
who wrote:

> Those who were just here saying farewell
> return to their homes. And though
>
> my family may still grieve, the others
> must be singing again by now. Once you're
>
> dead and gone, what then? Trust yourself
> to the mountainside. It will take you in.

Brooke wrote: "Wrestle with what you have to be
better and better and better." "Like Jacob and the
angel." She ended one of her last poems, *Biography of
Miss Go Chi*, this way:

> It is
> comforting
> to note
> that we are
>
> only
> images
> projected
> from afar.
>
> Our souls
> are in
> the stars

so if
a comet
destroys us
we will
survive

and our
stories
will be on
the air.

There's nothing we can say
to the universe when one we loved
departs, except to notice the new star
in the sky and realize that we know its name.

Written for and read at
Brooke's memorial service,
January 21, 2018, Katonah, N.Y.

T'ao Yüan-ming: His other name was T'ao Ch'ien. Excerpt from "Burial Songs," *The Selected Poems of Tao Ch'ien*, translated by David Hinton (Port Townsend, Washington: Copper Canyon Press, 1993), 83.

PUBLISHER'S NOTES

M. B. GOFFSTEIN studied Chinese in 1962, after graduating from Bennington College. Her teacher at the University of Minnesota, Dr. Lu, gave her the name Miss Go Chi. It was the closest Dr. Lu could come to the sound of Goffstein in Chinese. As Brooke progressed, the teacher told her that she spoke as well as a five-year-old, a compliment Brooke treasured.

In the early 1960s, Brooke moved to New York City, near Columbia University on 113th Street. In a bookstore, she discovered *The White Pony: An Anthology of Chinese Poetry* (edited by Robert Payne, New York: John Day, 1947) and these lines from "Seeing Hsia Chan Off by River" by Po Chü-i:

> *Homeless at seventy*
> *wind rise boat sail*
> *white-headed man*
> *white-headed wave*

This began a lifelong love for the great Chinese poets.

Some years before her death, Brooke wrote about her own afterlife as Miss Go Chi, herself transformed. The initial title was *Miss Go Chi in Heaven*. She later decided on *Biography of Miss Go Chi* and shared the manuscript-in-progress with visitors at the hospice almost until the day she passed.

Similarly, *Mario's Garage* was a long-term project about the afterlife. It is not explicitly stated, but *Mario's* is the all-night garage in North Bennington, mentioned in *Biography of Miss Go Chi*, where Miss Go buys her peanuts.

Noveletto is a word Brooke invented to mean a short, confectionary style of novel, written in the condensed style of poetry. The word was an homage to Walnettos, a candy made in Minnesota.

Her first novelettos were written around 2000, set in and around Rena Rosenfeld's old shop in the Waldorf. As the stories went on, the characters ended up in heaven, and that led to the realization that, for her, heaven was the progressive all-girls Bennington College in the years she was a student.

In Brooke's cosmology (a grander word than she would have used), the first ring of heaven is a bazaar with flea markets and thrift shops. There, a person can choose something to send back to earth for a loved one. Beyond the bazaar, heaven is a place of endless possibility.

•

The text of *Days and Nights at Our Prairie Home* is drawn from one published work, *Our Prairie Home: A Picture Album*, and one unpublished manuscript, *New Prairie Home*.

The handyman at Presidents Lodge, Joe in "Up at the Lake," and Joe Denton in *Boiled Rice Mountain*, may be the same person seen from very different perspectives.

•

Acknowledgments in the original edition of *Our Prairie Home: A Picture Album*: Hello to Iris Brown and Ken Hanson. Thanks always to C. Z., John Vitale, Abby Sundell, Antonia Market, Alan Horowitz, and Constance Fogler.

•

Two of M. B. Goffstein's recurring characters appear in *Boiled Rice Mountain*. For more about Daisy Summerfield and Paula Nathanson, look for *Art Girls Together: Two Novels* and *Daisy Summerfield's Art*, both by M. B. Goffstein.

•

The *Life* magazine article that was the basis for *Love and Dust* also is the basis for the "Alberto Giacometti" chapter in *Family Scrapbook*.

ACKNOWLEDGMENTS

VERY SPECIAL THANKS to
Linda Love, Ann Marie D'Agostino, Linda O'Shea of Awakenings in
Katonah, gone but maybe now a piece of Heaven;
Cheryl Weinstein;
Olga, Carlos, Carlitos, and Christian Ramirez-Lopez;
Bill Zavatsky and Doreen Stock;
Thacher, Olivia, and Nicholas Hurd;
Brooke's former students and colleagues especially Ed Miller, Joceline
Arsenault, Michelle Gengaro, Tanya Bylinsky Fabian, Tamar Taylor,
Kate Roeder, Kate Spohn, Gary Bilezikian, Amy Snyder;
Rachel Zucker for that day;
Brooke Koven for the text design and always being there;
all the staff and volunteers at the Regional Hospice Danbury, Connecticut.

THANKS TO EVERYONE at Girl Friday Productions, especially
the splendidly skilled and smart Karen McNally Upson, for guiding
this project through to its realization (Brooke would have *loffed* you!):

Editorial: Lisa L. Owens and Kelley Frodel
Design: Rachel Marek